Thomas Fuller

The Wit and Wisdom of Thomas Fuller

With a brief biography

Thomas Fuller

The Wit and Wisdom of Thomas Fuller
With a brief biography

ISBN/EAN: 9783337015732

Printed in Europe, USA, Canada, Australia, Japan

Cover: Foto ©Raphael Reischuk / pixelio.de

More available books at **www.hansebooks.com**

THE WIT AND WISDOM

OF

THOMAS FULLER

WITH A BRIEF BIOGRAPHY

THE RELIGIOUS TRACT SOCIETY

56, PATERNOSTER ROW; 65, ST. PAUL'S CHURCHYARD;
AND 164, PICCADILLY.

1886.

CONTENTS.

———◆◆◆———

BRIEF BIOGRAPHY OF
THOMAS FULLER.

'NEXT to Shakespeare,' writes Coleridge, 'I am not certain whether Thomas Fuller, beyond all other writers, does not excite in me the sense and emotion of the marvellous;—the degree in which any given faculty or combination of faculties is possessed and manifested, so far surpassing what one would have thought possible in a single mind, as to give one's admiration the flavour and quality of wonder! Wit was the stuff and substance of Fuller's intellect. It was the element, the earthen base, the material which he worked in; and this very circumstance has defrauded him of his due praise for the practical wisdom of the thoughts, for the beauty and variety of the truths, into which he shaped the stuff. Fuller was incomparably the most sensible, the least prejudiced, great man of an age that boasted a galaxy of great men. He is a very voluminous writer; and yet, in all his numerous volumes on so many different subjects, it is scarcely too much to say, that you will hardly find a page in which some one sentence out of every three does not deserve to be quoted for itself as motto or as maxim.'

Though Thomas Fuller was by no means a recluse student, and though he lived in one of the most eventful periods of our history, yet the recorded facts of his history are neither numerous nor important, and for the greater part of them the modern reader is indebted to Fuller's own works.

He was born in the year 1608, at Aldwinkle, in which village his father, a man of considerable learning, was rector. In his own quaint style he thus speaks of his birthplace. 'God in his providence fixed my nativity in a remarkable place. I was born at Aldwinkle, in Northamptonshire, where my father was the painful (painstaking) preacher of St. Peter's. This village was distanced one good mile west from Achurch, where Mr. Brown, founder of the Brownists, did dwell, whom, out of curiosity, when a youth I often visited. It was likewise a mile east from Lavender, where Francis Tresham, so active in the Gunpowder Treason, had a large demesne and ancient habitation. My nativity may remind me of moderation, whose cradle was rocked between two rocks. Now, seeing that I was never such a churl as to desire to eat my morsel alone, let such who like my prayer join with me herein—God grant we may hit the golden mean, and endeavour to avoid all extremes; the fanatic Anabaptist on one side, the fiery zeal of the Jesuit on the other, that so we may be true Protestants, or, which is a far better name, real Christians in deed.'[1]

[1] Aldwinkle was likewise the birthplace of Dryden: and Dr. Haweis, one of the founders of the London Missionary Society, was incumbent of the parish.

At the early age of twelve, having attended a village school for four years, he was sent to Cambridge, and entered at Queen's College. Dr. Davenant, afterwards Bishop of Salisbury, his maternal uncle, was the master, and his cousin, Edward Davenant, one of the tutors. He took his degree of B.A. in 1624-5, and M.A. in 1628. His relatives used all their influence, which was considerable, to secure his preferment, and he speedily became Perpetual Curate of St. Bevis, Fellow of Sidney Sussex College, and Prebendary of Salisbury. Whilst incumbent of St. Bevis he delivered a course of lectures on the Book of Ruth, which he subsequently printed. In the year 1631, he published his first book. It was a poem, with the quaint alliterative title of *David's Hainous Sin, Heartie Repentance, and Heavy Punishment.* It is now quite forgotten, as, indeed, it deserves to be. Fuller did not possess the poetic ' gift and faculty divine.'

In 1634, he preached, and subsequently printed, a sermon on *The Doctrine of Assurance.* It affords an admirable illustration of the calmness, moderation, and scriptural soundness of his views. Fanatical extravagance on one side, and ritualistic, Romanizing tendencies on the other, had brought this doctrine in discredit. The one party spoke of assurance as essential to salvation, and as conferred by a special Divine illumination; the other rejected it altogether as mere enthusiasm. Steering between these two extremes, Fuller lays it down as the plain teaching of his text (2 Pet. i. 10), that assurance may be attained in this life without any miraculous revelation. But he strenuously insists that it can never be enjoyed by those who make their Christian profession a life of worldly conformity or luxurious ease. 'The grace of assurance,' he says, 'is not attainable with ease and idleness. Christianity is a laborious profession.'

Whilst he urges all his hearers to strive after its attainment and enjoyment, he is careful to show that true saving faith may be possessed without it. The two things are separable from one another. 'I say, separable, to manifest my dissenting from such worthy divines, who make this assurance to be the very being, essence, life, soul, and formality of faith itself. Whence these two opinions, as false as dangerous, must of necessity be inferred, first, that every one who hath true faith and is eternally to be saved hath *always* some measure of this assurance; secondly, that such who are devoid of this assurance, are likewise deprived of all sincere faith for the present. But God forbid any preacher should deliver doctrines so destructive to Christian comfort on the one side and advantageous to spiritual pride on the other. Such will prove *carnificinæ*, the racks and tortures of tender consciences. And as the careless mother killed her little child, for she overlaid it, so the weight of this heavy doctrine would press many poor but pious souls, many faint but feeble infant-faiths to the pit of despair; exacting and extorting from them more than God requires,—that every faith should have assurance with it, or else be ineffectual to salvation.'

Following the scholastic method then so popular, he proposed his argument in the form of a syllogism.

The Major—'He that truly repenteth himself of his sins, and relieth with a true faith upon Christ, is

surely called, and by consequence elected before all
eternity to be a vessel of honour.'

The Minor—'But I truly repent myself of my
sins, and rely with a true faith on God in Christ.'

The Conclusion—'Therefore I am truly called and
elected,' etc.

He shows that in order to attain this assurance we
must have, first, the testimony of a good conscience to
the reality of our repentance and the sincerity of our
faith; and secondly, the witness of the Holy Spirit
(Rom. viii. 16).

In meeting some of the objections which were urged
against this doctrine, he uses the following striking
and characteristic illustration :—'Now we must with
sorrow confess that this doctrine of the Spirit dwelling
in the hearts of God's servants, is much discounte-
nanced of late, and the devil thereupon hath improved his own interest. To speak plainly, it is not
the fierceness of the lion, nor the fraud of the fox,
but the mimicalness of the ape, which, in our age,
hath discredited the undoubted truth. But what if
the apes in India, finding a glow-worm, mistook it to
be true fire, and heaping much combustible matter
about it, hoped by their blowing of it, thence to
kindle a flame ; I say, what if that laughter-causing
animal, that mirth-making creature deceived itself,
doth it thence follow that there is no true fire at all?
And what if some fanatics by usurpation have entitled their brainsick fancies to be so many illumina-
tions of the Spirit, must we presently turn Sadducees
in this point, and deny that there is any Spirit at all?
God forbid.'

In replying to those who pretend that assurance of salvation would tend to a carnal and presumptuous security, he shows that the very reverse is the fact, and that the blessed effects of a well-founded assurance are amongst the proofs of its truth.

'The third and last witness we will insist on is that comfort and contentment the conscience of the party takes in doing good works, and bringing forth the fruits of new obedience; that though he knows his best good works are straitened with corruptions and many imperfections, yet because they are the end of his vocation, and the justifiers of his faith; because thereby the gospel is graced, wicked men amazed, some of them converted, the rest confounded, weak Christians confirmed, the poor relieved, devils repining at them, angels rejoicing for them, God himself glorified by them; I say, because of these and other reasons, he doth good deeds with humility and cheerfulness, and findeth a singular joy in his soul resulting from the doing thereof.'

He admits that many true believers never attain to this comfortable assurance, and that some who are self-deceivers never doubt their safety; but he maintains that godly sorrow will, as a rule, be accompanied by inward peace, that it will be followed by spiritual joy, and that it will fill our hearts with gratitude, our lips with praise. He admirably says, 'All heavenly gifts, as they are got by prayer, are kept, confirmed, and increased by praise.' Excellent, too, is the following caution against presumption and false security:—'Presumption is hot poison; it kills its thousands, makes quick riddance of men's souls to damnation. Despair, we confess, is poison, and hath killed its thousands, but the venom thereof is more curable, as more cold and faint in the operation thereof. Take heed, therefore, of presumption, lest the confidence of the assurance of thy calling betray thee to spiritual pride, that to security, that to destruction.'

If controverted doctrines had always been defended in this temper and spirit, polemical theology would not have been the opprobrium of the Church.

In the year 1634, he received, through the kindness of his uncle Davenant, the Rectory of Broad Windsor, in Dorsetshire, and in the following year returned to Cambridge, to take his degree of Bachelor of Divinity. It illustrates the affection with which his parishioners regarded him as well as the charm of his society that, 'at his setting forth, he was acquainted that four of his chief parishioners, with his good leave, were ready to wait on him to Cambridge, to testify their exceeding engagements; it being the sense and request of his whole parish. This kindness was so present and so resolutely pressed, that the Doctor, with many thanks for that and other demonstrations of their love towards him, gladly accepted of their company, and with his customary innate pleasantness entertained their time to the journey's end.'

On his return to Broad Windsor he set himself to complete the works which he had planned and commenced at Cambridge. The first of these was the *History of the Holy War*, the dedication of which, to Lord Montagu and Sir John Powlett, is dated March 6th, 1639. It is a clear, well-written, and learned history of the Crusades, and, at one period, was very popular.

It abounds with his peculiar quaintnesses of style, which enliven what in other hands would be a dry catalogue of names. Thus in enumerating the important towns in Palestine, he says : 'Aphek, whose walls falling down, gave both the death and grave-stones to twenty-seven thousand of Benhadad's soldiers.' 'Sisera, who for all his commanding nine hundred iron chariots, was slain with one iron nail.' 'Gibeon, whose inhabitants cozened Joshua with a pass of false-dated antiquity: who could have thought that clouted shoes could have covered so much subtilty!' 'Edrei, the city of Og, on whose giant-like proportions the Rabbies have invented more giant-like lies.' 'Gadara, whose inhabitants loved their swine better than their Saviour.' 'Pisgah, where Moses viewed the land ; hereabouts the angel buried him, and also buried the grave lest it should occasion idolatry.' 'The fountain where Bathsheba's washing her body occasioned the fouling of her soul.'

Whilst at Broad Windsor he married ; the precise date is uncertain, and of his wife little is known. His wedded life soon terminated by the death of his wife, leaving an infant son, who survived his father.

The strife between the King and the Parliament was now rapidly becoming embittered, and the clouds were gathering which were soon to break over the land in storm and tempest. In the year 1640, the memorable Convocation met at Westminster, which did so much to alienate the different parties in the Church. Of this Convocation Fuller was a member, and acted during part of the time as secretary. Dissatisfied with the course of events, however, he joined with a number of members who protested against the course of the dominant party, and withdrew. In his _Church History_ and _Appeal of Injured Innocence_ he has left a minute account of the proceedings of the Convocation, and of his own share in them. These transactions, however, belong rather to ecclesiastical history than to the biography of Fuller, and need no further notice here.

In the same year (1640), he contributed a sermon to a volume of funeral discourses, entitled _Threnikos, The House of Mourning furnished_; and a volume which he called _Joseph's parti-coloured coat_. In the sermon, which is upon Rom. xii. 2, occurs the following passage, the fidelity of which is worthy of all praise:—'I know, and see by daily experience everywhere, how few there be that in their lifetime deserve the praise of religion in their death. For my part, I never did, nor never will gild a rotten post or a mud wall, or give false witness in praising, to give the praise of religion to those that deserve it not. I desire those of my congregation would make their own funeral sermons while they be living, by their virtuous life and conversation. As the Apostle saith, "He hath not praise that is praised of men, but he that is praised of God."'

Joseph's parti-coloured coat is a volume of expository discourses, distinguished by all Fuller's vigour, piety, and wit. It abounds with quaint, pithy, epigrammatic sayings, such as 'Practice without knowledge is blind; knowledge without practice is lame.' 'To him, to whom the sacrament is not heaven, it is hell.' 'What was pride in the builders of Babel will be piety in us, to mount and raise our souls on high till the top of them reach to heaven.' Longer extracts from this work will be found amongst the selections in the present volume.

In 1641, Fuller removed to London, where he was appointed to the · Lectureship of the Savoy. His preaching seems to have been very popular, especially amongst the lawyers and barristers at the Inns of Court. In the numerous dedications prefixed to the chapters of his *Church History, British Worthies,* and *Pisgah-sight of Palestine,* he commemorates the names of many, eminent for learning and piety, whose friendship he had formed at this period.

It was whilst preaching at the Savoy that he published the *Holy and Profane State,* perhaps his best known and most popular work. It consists of a series of brief biographies and sketches of character, admirable for their vivacity of style and accuracy of delineation. Extracts are given from this work in the following pages.

Hitherto he had quietly pursued the 'even tenour of his way,' faithfully preaching the gospel, and avoiding . all cause of offence with any party in the State. But it was difficult, perhaps impossible, in those stormy and troubled times, to remain on friendly terms with the opposing factions. Fuller, though both by nature and from conviction a lover of moderation and of peace, was not the man to conceal or modify his own views of truth and duty. And it happened to him, as it commonly happens to those who in times of revolution 'seek peace and ensue it,' that he gave offence to both parties. In the year 1643, he preached at Westminster Abbey, on the anniversary of the King's accession. He chose as his text the words in 2 Sam. xix. 30, 'And Mephibosheth said unto the king, Yea, let him take all, forasmuch as my lord the king is come again in peace unto his own house.' The sermon was a characteristic exhortation to mutual confidence and good feeling. He urged upon the contending parties the duty of seeking peace as the object of all their endeavours. 'There must,' he says, 'at last be a mutual confiding on both sides, so that they must count the honesty of others their only hostages. This the sooner it be done, the easier it is done. For who can conceive that when both sides have suffered more wrongs they will sooner forgive, or when they have offered more wrongs be sooner forgiven? For our King's part, let us demand of his money what Christ asked of Cæsar's coin—Whose image is this? *Charles's:* and what is the superscription? *Religio Protestantium, Leges Angliæ, Libertates Parliamenti:* [1] and he hath caused them to be cast both in silver and gold, in pieces of several sizes and proportions; as if thereby to show that he intends to make good his promise both to poor and rich, great and small, and we are bound to believe him.

'Nor less fair are the professions of the Parliament on the other side, and no doubt but as really they intend them. But these matters belong not to us to meddle with, and as for all other politic objections

[1] The religion of Protestants, the laws of England, the liberties of Parliament.

against peace, they pertain not to the pulpit to answer. All that we desire to see, is the King re-married to the State; and we doubt not, but as the bridegroom, on the one side, will be careful to have his portion paid, *his prerogative;* so the bride's friends, entrusted to her, will be sure to see her jointure settled—*the liberty of the subject.'*

Towards the conclusion of his sermon he enforced the duty of prayer — special, fervent, importunate prayer—that God would overrule the events of the time for the nation's welfare and his own glory. 'Let us pray faithfully, pray fervently, pray constantly, pray continually. Let preacher and people join their prayers together, that God would be pleased to build up the walls and make up the breaches in the application, that what cannot be told, may be foretold for a truth; and that our text may be verified of Charles in prophecy, as by David in history. Excellently St. Austin adviseth, that men should not be curious to inquire how original sin came into them, but careful to seek how to get it out. By the same similitude (though reversed) let us not be curious to know what made our King to leave this city, or whether offences given or taken moved him to his departure; but let us bend our brains, and improve our best endeavours to bring him safely and speedily back again. How often herein have our pregnant hopes miscarried, even when they were to be delivered! Just as a man in a storm, swimming through the sea to the shore, till the oars of his faint arms begin to fail him, is now come to catch land, when an unmerciful wave beats him as far back in an instant as he can recover in an hour:

just so when our hopes of a happy peace have been ready to arrive, some envious unexpected obstacle hath started up, and hath set our hopes ten degrees backwards, as the shadow of the sun-dial of Ahaz. But let us not hereat be disheartened, but with blind Bartimeus, the more we are commanded by unhappy accidents to hold our peace, let us cry the louder in our prayers, the rather, because our King is already partly come, come in his offer to come, come in his tender to treat, come in his proffer of peace. And this very day, being the beginning of the treaty, I may say he set his first step forward: God guide his feet, and speed his pace. O let us thriftily husband the least mite of hopes that it may increase, and date our day from the first peeping of the morning star, before the sun be risen. In a word, desist from sinning, persist in praying, and then it may come to pass that this our use may once be antedated, and this day's sermon sent as a harbinger beforehand to provide a lodging in your hearts for your joy against the time, that "my lord our king shall return to his own house in peace."'

These were wise and weighty words. But we, who judge after the event, can see how hopeless were all such attempts at pacification. The disease in the body-politic was too severe and too deeply rooted to be eradicated without some violent measures.

The discourse gave great offence to the more extreme partisans who heard it. Shortly after this he was called upon, together with the other London clergy, to take an oath of allegiance to the Parliament. 'This,' he says, ' was tendered to me and taken by

me in the vestry of the Savoy Church, but first pro-
testing some limitations thereof to myself. This, not
satisfying, was complained of, by some persons present,
to the Parliament; where it was ordered, that the
next Lord's day I should take the same oath *in
terminis terminantibus*, in the face of the Church;
which not agreeing with my conscience, I withdrew
myself into the King's parts.'

He seems to have found himself as little at home
with the Royalists in Oxford as with the Parliament-
arians in London. Being called upon to preach before
the King, his sermon gave great offence to the zealots
of his own party, to whom his moderation and impar-
tiality were very distasteful. After a stay of only
three months in Lincoln College, Oxford, he applied
for and received a chaplaincy in the army, under Lord
Hopton. There were few of the officers in the King's
service to whom a man of Fuller's character would
have been acceptable, or under whom he could have
served. Lord Hopton, however, and his Chaplain
seem to have been in perfect accord. Fuller's anony-
mous biographer says of him, 'This noble lord, though
as courageous and expert a captain, and successful
withal as any the King had, was never averse to an
amicable closure of the war upon fair and honourable
terms, and did, therefore, well approve of the Doctor
and his desires and pursuit after peace. The good
Doctor was likewise infinitely contented in his attendance on such an excellent personage, whose conspicuous and noted loyalty could not but derive the
same reputation to his retainers, especially one so
near to his conscience as his Chaplain.'

We do not need the testimony of his admiring biographer to assure us that Fuller was indefatigable in the duties of his chaplaincy, that he read the liturgy with the troops under his charge daily, and preached every Sunday. Whilst attached to Lord Hopton's regiment he formed part of the garrison of Basing House at the time of its celebrated siege by Sir William Waller. The successful defence against the Parliamentary forces seems to have been in great part due to the animating and vigorous exhortations which Fuller addressed to the troops.

Fuller turned to good account the constant change of place which the duties of his chaplaincy involved. Marching and counter-marching through the southern and eastern counties of England, he employed himself in collecting materials for his great work, *The Worthies of England.* It was not published till 1662, the year after his own death, when it appeared as a folio, edited by his son. It is a work of great research and permanent value, though the whimsical episodes and antiquarian gossip in which it abounds often raise a smile at the author's expense.

In the year 1644, Fuller left the army, and took up his abode in Exeter. He here received the honorary appointment of Chaplain to the infant princess Henrietta Maria, was presented to the living of Dorchester, and published his *Good Thoughts in Bad Times*, and two years later (1647) his *Good Thoughts in Worse Times*. These are perhaps his most generally popular treatises, and are given almost *in extenso* (pp. 35–127).

In his *Worthies of England* he records the following

remarkable occurrence as having happened whilst he resided in Exeter during its siege by Sir Thomas Fairfax :—

'When the city of Exeter was besieged by the Parliament forces, so that only the south side thereof towards the sea was open unto it, incredible numbers of larks were found in that open quarter, for multitude like quails in the wilderness, though (blessed be God) unlike them both in cause and effect, as not desired with man's destruction, nor sent with God's anger, as appeared by their safe digestion into wholesome nourishment. Hereof I was an eye and mouth witness. I will save my credit in not conjecturing any number; knowing that herein, though I should stoop below the truth, I should mount above belief. They were as fat as plentiful; so that being sold for two pence a dozen and under, the poor (who could have no cheaper, as the rich no better meat) used to make pottage of them, boiling them down therein. Several natural causes were assigned hereof. . . . However, the cause of causes was Divine Providence, thereby providing a feast for many poor people who otherwise had been pinched for provision.'

When Exeter fell into the hands of the Parliament, Fuller returned to London, and became Lecturer, first at St. Clement's, Lombard Street,[1] then at St. Bride's,

---

[1] Mr. Russell, author of *Memorials of the Life and Works of Thomas Fuller*, has disinterred from the Churchwardens' accounts for April, 1647, the following entry, which is curious as illustrating the scale of ministerial remuneration at that period:—*Paid for four sermons preached by Mr. ffuller*, £001 06, 08.

Fleet Street. He did not hold these appointments long, for, as a known Royalist, he was silenced by the dominant party in the State. But he could not be idle, and he employed his enforced leisure in preparing his *Pisgah-sight of Palestine and the Confines thereof, with the history of the Old and New Testament acted thereon,* forming a folio of about 700 pages, which appeared in 1650.

After a brief interval, we again find Fuller preaching without let or hindrance, the prohibition being meant to apply chiefly to political offenders. He was summoned to appear before the Court of Triers, who were appointed to examine all ministers and remove such as they found ignorant, incompetent, or vicious. Fuller was in some doubt as to how he should succeed in passing the scrutiny of the examiners, and applied to John Howe for help and advice, to whom he said, 'Sir, you may observe that I am a pretty corpulent man, and I am to go through a passage that is very strait; I beg you would be so good as to give me a shove and help me through.' Howe gave him all the assistance in his power. When called before the Triers, they asked him, 'Whether he had ever had any experience of a work of grace in his heart?' Fuller replied that 'He could appeal to the Searcher of all hearts that he made a conscience of his very thoughts.' This answer was deemed so satisfactory that, backed as it doubtless was by the friendly support of Howe, no further questions were asked him, and he was duly authorized to preach. The examiners requested him, before he left, to give them some proof of his extraordinary memory. With the quaint humour which never forsook him, he replied, that if they would restore a poor sequestered minister, he would never forget their kindness as long as he lived.

It speaks well, both for the courage of Fuller and for the moderation of Parliament, that one use he made of his restored liberty of speech was to preach, at Chelsea, a funeral sermon for the king. He did not, it is true, mention the name of the monarch, but no one could mistake the reference to Charles. The sermon was entitled *The Just Man's Funeral,* and was 'a vindication of the Divine Providence in the misfortunes and deaths of the righteous.' His explanation of the word righteous may serve to show how thoroughly Scriptural and evangelical were his views. He says the word is used of good men, *comparatively* in reference to the wicked; *intentionally,* inasmuch as they desire and endeavour after righteousness with all their might; *inhesively,* as having implanted within them heavenly graces and holy endowments, which are sincere though imperfect; and *imputatively,* as having the righteousness of Christ imputed to them.[1]

He now settled at Waltham, to the perpetual curacy of which he had been appointed by the Earl of Carlisle, whose Chaplain he was. Whilst at Waltham he passed through the press his *Pisgah-*

---

[1] The same thought is carried out at considerable length in a sermon preached a few years afterwards from Psalm xxxvii. 37, in which he lays great stress upon the imputed righteousness of Christ.

sight, to which reference has already been made, was a large contributor to a volume of biographies of the martyrs and confessors, called *Abel Redivivus,* and published many discourses, expositions of Scripture, and small treatises, amongst which was a defence of the baptism of infants, under the title of the *Infant's Advocate.* In 1654, Fuller married again. His second wife was a sister of Lord Baltinglass, and a great-granddaughter of Bishop Pilkington, by whom he had one son.

Two years later, he published his great work, *The Church History of Britain from the birth of Jesus Christ until the year* 1648 : *Endeavoured by Thomas Fuller.* It originally formed a large folio, and has frequently been reprinted. The last edition consists of three octavo volumes of between 500 and 600 pages each, with a supplemental volume, containing the *Histories of Cambridge and of Waltham Abbey,* and the *Appeal of Injured Innocence,* making nearly 700 pages more. These books, poured forth in such rapid succession, were all of a nature to require immense research, and they display the varied knowledge and indomitable industry of their author. Even had they been produced by one who had no interruption to his studies, no anxieties upon his mind, and who enjoyed all facilities for prosecuting his researches, they would still remain a marvellous monument of indefatigable diligence. But his position was the very reverse of this. Often and pathetically he laments the difficulties with which he had to contend. Yet even here his quaint humour constantly breaks through. Thus, in the preface to the

Appeal of Injured Innocence, he says, 'For the last five years, during our actual civil wars, I had little list or leisure to write; fearing to be myself made a history, and shifting daily for my safety. All that time I could not live to study, who did only study to live.' Again, in the preface to his *Church History*, he says, 'This history is now, though late (all Church work is slow), brought with much difficulty to an end. The first three books of this volume were for the main written in the reign of the late king. The other nine books were made since *monarchy* was turned into a *state*.'

The *Church History* was written by Fuller in a spirit of true charity, and with a warm sympathy for evangelical teaching. It, in consequence, gave great offence to the Romanizing party in the Church, who denounced Fuller as a puritan in disguise, and charged upon him as a fault that he held up to condemnation the superstitions and malpractices of the papacy. Heylin especially made a very fierce attack upon him on this ground. He, however, found more than his match in Fuller, who replied in one of the most remarkable controversial pamphlets in the language —*The Appeal of Injured Innocence*. It is brimful of wit, learning, and logic, and leaves Heylin utterly discomfited.

The restoration of Charles II. to the throne ended the troubles of Fuller, and placed him in the high road to promotion. But it came too late to enable him to reap the full rewards of his labours. He was restored to his lectureship at the Savoy and to his Prebendal stall at Salisbury, was appointed Chaplain

Extraordinary to the King, and received the degree of
D.D. by royal mandate. There was little doubt that
he would have been speedily raised to the bench, but
his end was near.

In August, 1661, he engaged to preach a wedding-
sermon at the Savoy, for a relative who was to be
married the next day. At dinner he complained of
feeling unwell. On being pressed by his son not to
preach, he replied that he had 'often gone up into
the pulpit sick, but always came down well again, and
he hoped he should do as well now, through God's
strengthening grace.' Whilst in the pulpit he felt
himself growing worse, and became apprehensive of
danger. With a foreboding of the result, he said to
the congregation, 'I find myself very ill, but I am
resolved by the grace of God to preach this sermon to
you, though it may be my last.' Bracing himself up
to the effort, he offered prayer and preached extempo-
raneously, as was his custom, with his usual point
and vigour, except that once in the middle of the
sermon he faltered, but speedily recovered himself.
The effort was his last. He was unable to rise from
his seat in the pulpit, and was with some difficulty
conveyed home. He soon after became unconscious,
but the day before his death ' it pleased God to restore
to him the use of his faculties, which he very devoutly
and thankfully employed in a Christian preparation
for death, earnestly imploring the prayers of some of
his reverend brethren with him, himself most intently
joining with them, and commending himself to the
will of God. Nay, so highly was he affected with
God's pleasure concerning him, that he could not

endure any person to weep or cry, but would earnestly desire them to refrain; highly extolling and preferring his condition, as a translation to a blessed eternity. Nor would he revert to subjects of a literary or purely secular kind: nothing but heaven and the perfections thereof, the consummation of grace in glory, must fill up the room of his capacious soul, now ready to take its flight from this world. On the morning of Thursday, the sixteenth of August, his sufferings were at an end, and he entered into rest.'

In person Fuller was tall and robust, with bright blue eyes, fresh ruddy complexion, and light curly hair. In diet he was sparing and temperate, in 'drink very much abstemious, which, questionless, was the cause of that uninterrupted health he enjoyed till his first and last sickness.' He allowed himself little time for recreation, and was especially moderate in sleep. Had he not carefully husbanded his time it would have been impossible for him to have produced a succession of volumes which form a library of themselves.

Reference has been made in the preceding pages to Fuller's extraordinary memory. Many of the mnemonic feats recorded of him almost surpass belief. It is said, for instance, that he could repeat five hundred strange words after once hearing them; that having once heard a sermon he could preach it over again verbatim; and that, on one occasion, he undertook, 'in passing to and fro from Temple Bar to the furthest conduit in Cheapside, to tell on his return every sign, as they stood in order on both sides of the way, repeating them backwards or forwards as they

should choose, which he exactly did, not missing or dis-
placing one, to the admiration of those that heard him.'

In a passage already quoted, Coleridge remarks that
Fuller's reputation for wit has 'defrauded him of his
due praise for the practical wisdom of his thoughts.'
The justice of this observation will be apparent in the
following selections. Passages of rare beauty, of deep
insight, of devout piety, and of tender pathos, will be
found in all his writings. This is especially the case
in his *Cause and Cure of a Wounded Conscience*, a
treatise of great value, though little known. The concluding sentences have a tender beauty, a soft and
pensive rhythm, which have been seldom surpassed.
Another passage, scarcely inferior to this in pathetic
beauty, may be found in the same treatise, describing
Adam in Paradise after his fall.

Professor Rogers, in his essay on the *Life and
Writings of Thomas Fuller*, after quoting Barrow's
comprehensive definition of wit, proceeds to show how
all its forms and varieties are exemplified by Fuller, and
gives us amongst others the following instances :—

'Speaking of the Jesuits, he says, "such is the
charity of the Jesuits, that they never owe any man
any ill-will—making present payment thereof." Of
certain prurient canons, in which virtue is in imminent danger of being tainted by impure descriptions
of purity, he shrewdly remarks—"One may justly
admire how these canonists, being pretended virgins,
could arrive at the knowledge of the criticisms of all
obscenity." Touching the miraculous coffin in which
St. Audré was deposited, he slyly says—"Under the
ruined walls of Grantchester or Cambridge, a coffin

was found, with a cover correspondent, both of white marble, which did fit her body so exactly, as if (which one may believe was true) it was *made* for it." On Machiavel's saying, " that he who undertakes to write a history must be of no religion," he observes, "if so, Machiavel himself was the best qualified of any in his age to be a good historian." On the unusual conjunction of great learning and great wealth in the case of Selden, he remarks, "Mr. Selden had some coins of the Roman emperors, and a great many more of our English kings." After commenting on the old story of St. Dunstan's pinching the devil's nose with the red-hot tongs, he drolly cries out—"But away with all suspicions and queries. None need to doubt of the truth thereof, finding it in a sign painted in Fleet Street, near Temple Bar." The bare, bald style of the schoolmen, he tells us, some have attributed to design "lest any of the vermin of equivocation should hide themselves under the *nap* of their words." On excessive attention to fashion in dress, he says—" Had some of our gallants been with the Israelites in the wilderness, when for forty years their clothes waxed not old, they would have been vexed, though their clothes were whole, to have been so long in one fashion." Speaking of the melancholy forebodings which have sometimes haunted the death-bed of good men, he quaintly tells us, "that the devil is most busy in the last day of his term, and a tenant to be *outed*, cares not what mishief he does." Of unreasonable expectations he says, with characteristic love of quibbling, "Those who *expect* what in reason they *cannot* expect, *may* expect." The court jester he wittily and truly characterizes thus—"It is an office which none but he that hath wit *can* perform, and none but he that wants wit *will* perform." Of modest women, who nevertheless dress themselves in questionable attire, he says—"I must confess some honest women may go thus, but no whit the honester for going thus. That ship may have Castor and Pollux for the sign, which, notwithstanding, has St. Paul for the lading." He thus speaks of anger—"He that keepeth anger long in his bosom, giveth place to the Devil. And why should we make room for him who will crowd in too fast of himself? Heat of passion makes our souls to crack, and the Devil creeps in at the crannies." Of intellectual deficiencies in the very *tall*, he remarks, "that oft-times such who are built four stories high, are observed to have little in their cock-loft." Of virtue in a very *short* man, he says, "His soul had but a short diocese to visit, and therefore might the better attend the effectual informing thereof."

'Of the "quirkish reason," mentioned as one of the species of wit in the above-recited passage of Barrow, the pages of our author are full. What can be more ridiculous than the reason he assigns, in his description of the "good wife," for the *order* of Paul's admonitions to husbands and wives in the third chapter of the Epistle to the Colossians? "The apostle first adviseth women to submit themselves to their husbands, and then counselleth men to love their wives. And sure it was fitting that women should first have their lesson given them, because it is hardest to be learned, and therefore they need have the more time to con it. For the same reason we first begin with the character of a good wife." Not less droll, or rather far more so, is the manner in which he subtilizes on the command, that we are not "to let the sun go down on our wrath." "Anger kept till the next morning, with manna, doth putrefy and corrupt; save that manna, corrupted not at all (and anger most of all), kept the next Sabbath. St. Paul saith, 'Let not the sun go down on your wrath,' to carry news to the antipodes in another world of thy revengeful nature. Yet let us take the apostle's meaning rather than his words, with all possible speed to depose our passion; not understanding him literally, so that we may take leave to be angry till sunset; then might our wrath lengthen with the days, and men in Greenland, where day lasts above a quarter of a year, have plentiful scope for revenge."'

Such instances as these might be multiplied almost indefinitely. Indeed, it would be difficult to open any of his treatises, except those of a devotional character, without meeting with some quaint or witty term at the first glance; and so inveterate was this habit in Fuller's mind, that it constantly crops out where we should least expect or desire it.

It must, indeed, be admitted that the tendency to jest and drollery was excessive. A sober and candid criticism must regard it as a defect in Fuller's character and a blemish in his style. Two or three considerations may, however, be urged, not, indeed, in justification, but in palliation. First, it should be remembered that it was perfectly natural to him. To have written in any other style would have called for constant restraint. Few things are more offensive than an affectation of, or a striving after, witty terms and amusing allusions. From this affected and artificial jocularity Fuller was entirely free. It should, further, be borne in mind that his wit was merely the outward form in which sound sense, serious purpose, and practical piety embodied themselves. In so far as it was a defect, it belonged rather to style, and manner, and mode of treatment, than to the stuff and substance of his thoughts. It may be compared with the pedantry which led some of his contemporaries to fill their pages with quotations from classical authors, or allusions to recondite facts; with the stiff scholasticism which led others to express their simplest statements in syllogistic and logical formulas; or with the tedious verbosity in which others indulged, expatiating in endless divisions and refinements, hair-splitting definitions and wire-drawn conclusions. The theologians and divines of that age were great, and their works possess a permanent value, not in consequence of these defects of style, but in spite of them. Let Fuller's excessive, and sometimes wearisome, jocularity find the same excuse. He, at least, is never pedantic, formal, or dull.

Fuller himself has prescribed the limits within which jesting is allowable, and it must be conceded to him that very seldom, if ever, has he outstepped them. His wit was never bitter and unkind, never profligate, never profane. He says, in his *Holy and Profane State* :—

'Harmless mirth is the best cordial against the consumption of the spirits; wherefore jesting is not unlawful if it trespasseth not in quantity, quality, or season.

B

'*Jest not with the two-edged sword of God's word.*
Will nothing please thee to wash thy hands in but
the font? or to drink healths in but the church-
chalice? And know that the whole art is learnt at
the first admission, and profane jests come without
calling. * * * Dangerous it is to wit-wanton it with
the majesty of God. Wherefore, if without thine
intention, and against thy will, by chance-medley
thou hittest Scripture in thy ordinary discourse, yet
fly to the city of refuge and pray God to forgive thee.

'*Wanton jests make fools laugh and wise men
frown.* Seeing we are civilized Englishmen, let us
not be naked savages in our talk.

'*Scoff not at the natural defects of any which are
not in their power to amend.* O! it is cruel to beat a
cripple with his crutches! Neither flout any for his
profession, if honest, though poor and painful.

'*He that relates another man's wicked jest with
delight adopts it to be his own.* Purge them therefore
from their poison. If the profaneness may be severed
from the wit, it is like lamprey—take out the sting, it
may make good meat. But if the staple-conceit consist in profaneness, then it is a viper, all poison: meddle
not with it.

'*He that will lose his friend for a jest deserves to die
a beggar by the bargain.* Yet some think their conceits
like mustard, not good except they bite. Such let thy
jests be that they grind not the credit of thy friend.'

If further apology be needed for Fuller, let it be
found in the concluding words of his preface to the
History of the Holy War: 'MAY THE FAULTS OF THIS
BOOK REDOUND TO MYSELF, THE PROFIT TO OTHERS,
THE GLORY TO GOD.'

GOOD THOUGHTS IN BAD TIMES

AND

GOOD THOUGHTS IN WORSE TIMES

CONSISTING OF

PERSONAL MEDITATIONS, SCRIPTURE OBSERVATIONS, HIS-
TORICAL APPLICATIONS, MIXED CONTEMPLATIONS,
MEDITATIONS ON ALL KINDS OF PRAYERS, AND OCCA-
SIONAL MEDITATIONS.

In the year 1645, Fuller was at Exeter. The Royal cause, to which he had attached himself, was rapidly becoming desperate. Moderate men of all parties were beginning to despair of any satisfactory or peaceful settlement of the questions at issue. Fuller, who had now retired from his military chaplaincy, employed his leisure in preparing and publishing his *Good Thoughts in Bad Times*. It was dedicated to Lady Dalkeith, governess to the infant Princess Henrietta, to whom he had received the appointment of Honorary Chaplain.

Two years later, in 1647, he published a second series of meditations, entitled *Good Thoughts in Worse Times*, similar in style, subject, and arrangement to the first series. They were exceedingly popular, and went through six or seven editions within a very few years.

Some years later, in 1660, he published a third series of meditations, entitled *Mixed Contemplations in Better Times*. The first and second series are given almost *in extenso*. A few meditations have been omitted which, referring to the controversies of the day, possessed only a temporary interest.

GOOD THOUGHTS IN BAD TIMES.

Commune with your own heart upon your bed, and be still.
—PSALM iv. 4.

PERSONAL MEDITATIONS.

LORD, how near was I to danger, yet escaped? I was upon the brink of the brink of it, yet fell not in; they are well kept who are kept by thee. Excellent archer! Thou didst hit the mark in missing it, as meaning to fright, not hurt me. Let me not now be such a fool as to pay my thanks to blind fortune for a favour which the eye of Providence hath bestowed upon me. Rather let the narrowness of my escape make my thankfulness to thy goodness the larger, lest my ingratitude justly cause that whereas this arrow but hit my hat, the next pierce my head.

*   *   *

LORD, when thou shalt visit me with a sharp disease I fear I shall be impatient, for I am choleric by my nature, and tender by my temper, and have not been acquainted with sickness all my lifetime. I cannot expect any kind usage from that which hath been a stranger unto me. I fear I shall rave and rage. O whither will my mind sail when distemper shall steer it? whither will my fancy run when diseases shall ride it? My tongue, which of itself is a fire

(James iii. 6), sure will be a wild-fire when the furnace of my mouth is made seven times hotter with a burning fever. But, Lord, though I should talk idly to my own shame, let me not talk wickedly to thy dishonour. Teach me the art of patience whilst I am well, and give me the use of it when I am sick. In that day either lighten my burthen or strengthen my back. Make me, who so often in my health have discovered my weakness presuming on my own strength, to be strong in sickness, when I solely rely on thy assistance.

* * *

LORD, this morning my unseasonable visiting of a friend disturbed him in the midst of his devotions: unhappy to hinder another man's goodness! If I myself build not, shall I snatch the axe and hammer from him that doth? yet I could willingly have wished that rather than he should then have cut off the cable of his prayers, I had twisted my cord to it, and joined with him in his devotions; however, to make him the best amends I may, I now request of thee for him whatsoever he would have requested for himself. Thus he shall be no loser if thou be pleased to hear my prayer for him, and to hearken to our Saviour's intercession for us both.

* * *

LORD, since these woeful wars began, one, formerly mine intimate acquaintance, is now turned a stranger, yea, an enemy. Teach me how to behave myself towards him. Must the new foe quite jostle out the old friend? may I not with him continue some commerce of kindness? though the amity be broken on his side, may not I preserve my counterpart entire? Yet how can I be kind to him without being cruel to myself and thy cause? O guide my shaking hand to draw so small a line straight; or rather because I know not how to carry myself towards him in this controversy, even be pleased to take away the subject of the question, and speedily to reconcile these unnatural differences.

* * *

LORD, my voice by nature is harsh and untunable, and it is vain to lavish any art to better it. Can my singing of psalms be pleasing to thy ears which is unpleasant to my own? yet though I cannot chant with the nightingale, or chirp with the blackbird, I had rather chatter with the swallow (Isaiah xxxviii. 14), yea, rather croak with the raven, than be altogether silent. Hadst thou given me a better voice, I would have praised thee with a better voice. Now what my music wants in sweetness let it have in sense, singing praises with understanding. Yea, Lord, create in me a new heart (therein to make melody), (Ephes. v. 19), and I will be contented with my old voice, until, in thy due time, being admitted into the choir of heaven, I have another, more harmonious, bestowed upon me.

* * *

LORD, within a little time I have heard the same precept in sundry places and by several preachers pressed upon me. The doctrine seemeth to haunt my soul; whithersoever I turn it meets me. Surely this is from thy providence, and should be for my profit. Is it because I am an ill proficient in this point, that I must not turn over a new leaf, but am still kept to my old lesson? Peter was grieved because our Saviour said unto him the third time, 'Lovest thou me?' But I will not be offended at thy often inculcating the same precept. But rather conclude that I am much concerned therein, and that it is thy pleasure that the nail should be soundly fastened in me, which thou hast knocked in with so many hammers.

*   *   *

LORD, before I commit a sin, it seems to me so shallow that I may wade through it dry-shod from any guiltiness; but when I have committed it, it often seems so deep that I cannot escape without drowning. Thus I am always in extremities: either my sins are so small that they need not any repentance, or so great that they cannot obtain thy pardon. Lend me, O Lord, a reed out of thy sanctuary, truly to measure the dimension of my offences. But, O! as thou revealest to me more of my misery, reveal also more of thy mercy: lest if my wounds, in my apprehension, gape wider than thy tents,[1] my soul run out at them. If my badness seem bigger than thy goodness but one hair's breadth, but one moment, that is room and time enough for me to run to eternal despair.

*   *   *

LORD, I do discover a fallacy whereby I have long deceived myself, which is this—I have desired to begin my amendment from my birthday, or from the first day of the year, or from some eminent festival, that so my repentance might bear some remarkable date. But when those days were come I have

[1] A plug of lint, placed in wounds to stop the bleeding.

adjourned my amendment to some other time. Thus whilst I could not agree with myself when to start, I have almost lost the running of the race. I am resolved thus to befool myself no longer. I see no day like to-day, the instant time is always the fittest time. In Nebuchadnezzar's image, the lower the members, the coarser the metal; the farther off the time, the more unfit. To-day is the golden opportunity, to-morrow will be the silver season, next day but the brazen one, and so long, till at last I shall come to the toes of clay, and be turned to dust. Grant, therefore, that to-day I may hear thy voice. And if this day be obscure in the calendar, and remarkable in itself for nothing else, give me to make it memorable in my soul, thereupon, by thy assistance, beginning the reformation of my life.

*   *   *

LORD, I saw one whom I knew to be notoriously bad in great extremity. It was hard to say whether his former wickedness or present want were the greater. If I could have made the distinction, I could willingly have fed his person and starved his profaneness. This being impossible, I adventured to relieve him. For I know that amongst many objects, all of them being in extreme miseries, charity, though shooting at random, cannot miss a right mark. Since, Lord, the party, being recovered, is become worse than ever before (thus they are always impaired with affliction, who thereby are not improved), Lord, count me not accessary to his badness because I relieved him. Let me not suffer harm in myself for my desire to do good to him. Yea, Lord, be pleased to clear my credit amongst men, that they may understand my hands according to the simplicity of my heart. I gave to him only in hope to keep the stock alive, that so afterwards it might be better grafted. Now, finding myself deceived, my alms shall return into my own bosom.

*　　*　　*

LORD, thy servants are now praying in the church, and I am here staying at home, detained by necessary occasions, such as are not of my seeking, but of thy sending. My care could not prevent them, my power could not remove them. Wherefore, though I cannot go to church, there to sit down at table with the rest of thy guests, be pleased, Lord, to send me a dish of their meat hither, and feed my soul with holy thoughts. Eldad and Medad (Numb. xi. 26), though staying still in the camp (no doubt on just cause), yet prophesied as well as the other elders. Though they went not out to the Spirit, the Spirit came home to them. Thus never any dutiful child lost his legacy for being absent at the making of his father's will, if at the same time he were employed about his father's business. I fear too many at church have their bodies there and minds at home. Behold, in exchange, my body here and heart there. Though I cannot pray with them, I pray for them. Yea, this comforts me, I *am* with thy congregation, because I *would* be with it.

*　　*　　*

LORD, I trust thou hast pardoned the bad examples I have set before others, be also pleased to pardon me the sins which they have committed by my bad examples. (It is the best manners in thy court to heap requests upon requests.) If thou hast forgiven my sins, the children of my corrupt nature, forgive me my grandchildren also. Let not the transcripts remain, since thou hast blotted out the original. . And for the time to come bless me with barrenness in bad actions, and my bad actions with barrenness, that they may never beget others according to their likeness.

* * *

LORD, what faults I correct in my son I commit myself: I beat him for dabbling in the dirt, whilst my own soul doth wallow in sin: I beat him for crying to cut his own meat, yet am not myself contented with that state thy providence hath carved unto me: I beat him for crying when he is to go to sleep, and yet I fear I myself shall cry when thou callest me to sleep with my fathers. Alas, I am more childish than my child, and what I inflict on him I justly deserve to receive from thee: only here is the difference. I pray and desire that my correction on my child may do him good. It is in thy power, Lord, to effect that thy correction on me shall do me good.

* * *

LORD, I perceive my soul deeply guilty of envy. By my good will, I would have none prophesy but mine own Moses (Numb. xi. 28). I had rather thy work were undone than done better by another than by myself! Had rather thy enemies were all alive than that I should kill but my thousand, and others their ten thousands of them! My corruption repines at other men's better parts, as if what my soul wants of them in substance she would supply in swelling. Dispossess me, Lord, of this bad spirit, and turn my envy into holy emulation. Let me labour to exceed them in pains who excel me in parts : and knowing that my sword in cutting down sin hath a duller edge, let me strike with the greater force ; yea, make other men's gifts to be mine, by making me thankful to thee for them. It was some comfort to Naomi, that, wanting a son herself, she brought up Ruth's child in her bosom. If my soul be too old to be a mother of goodness, Lord, make it but a dry-nurse. Let me feed and foster and nourish and cherish the graces in others, honouring their persons, praising their parts, and glorifying thy Name, who hath given such gifts unto them.

* * *

LORD, when young I have almost quarrelled with that petition, 'Give peace in our time, O Lord;' needless to wish for light at noon-day ; for then peace was so plentiful, no fear of famine, but suspicion of a surfeit thereof. And yet how many good comments was this prayer then capable of ! Give peace, that is, continue and preserve it ; give peace, that is, give us hearts worthy of it, and thankful for it. In our time, that is, all our time : for there is more besides a fair morning required to make a fair day. Now I see the mother had more wisdom than her son. The Church knew, better than I, how to pray. Now I am better informed of the necessity of that petition. Yea, with the daughters of the horseleech, I have need to cry, Give, give—peace in our time, O Lord (Prov. xxx. 15).

* * *

LORD, unruly soldiers command poor people to open

them their doors, otherwise threatening to break in. But if those in the house knew their own strength it were easy to keep them out; seeing the doors are threatening-proof, and·it is not the breath of their oaths can blow the locks open. Yet, silly souls, being affrighted, they obey, and betray themselves to their violence. Thus Satan serves me, or rather thus I serve myself. When I cannot be forced, I am fooled out of my integrity. He cannot constrain if I do not consent. If I do but keep possession, all the powers of hell cannot violently eject me: but I cowardly surrender to his summons. Thus there needs no more to my undoing, but myself.

* * *

LORD, when I am to travel I never use to provide myself till the very time; partly out of laziness, loth to be troubled till needs I must; partly out of pride, as presuming all necessaries for my journey will wait upon me at the instant (some say this is scholar's fashion, and it seems, by following it, I hope to approve myself to be one). However, it often comes to pass that my journey is finally stopped, through the narrowness of the time to provide for it. Grant, Lord, that my confessed improvidence in temporal may make me suspect my providence in spiritual matters. Solomon saith, 'Man goeth to his long home.' Short preparation will not fit so long a journey. O let me not put it off to the last, to have my oil to buy when I am to burn it, but let me so dispose of myself, that when I am to die I may have nothing to do but to die,

LORD, when in any writing I have occasion to insert these passages, God willing, God lending me life, etc., I observe, Lord, that I can scarce hold my hand from encircling these words in a parenthesis, as if they were not essential to the sentence, but may as well be left out as put in.   Whereas indeed they are not only of the commission at large, but so of the quorum, that without them all the rest is nothing; wherefore hereafter I will write those words fully and fairly, without any enclosure about them.   Let critics censure it for bad grammar, I am sure it is good divinity.

*   *   *

LORD, many temporal matters which I have desired, thou hast denied me.   It vexed me for the present, that I wanted my will.   Since, considering in cold blood, I plainly perceive had that which I desired been done, I had been undone.   Yea, what thou gavest me, instead of those things which I wished, though less toothsome to me, were more wholesome for me.   Forgive, I pray, my former anger, and now accept my humble thanks.   Lord, grant me one suit, which is this,—deny me all suits which are bad for me: when I petition for what is unfitting, O let the King of heaven make use of his negative voice.   Rather let me fast than have quails given with intent that I should be choked in eating them (Numb. xi. 33).

*   *   *

LORD, this day I disputed with myself whether or no I had said my prayers this morning; and I could not call to mind any remarkable passage whence I could certainly conclude that I had offered my prayers unto thee. Frozen affections, which left no spark of remembrance behind them! Yet at last I hardly recovered one token, whence I was assured that I had said my prayers. It seems I had said them, and only said them, rather by heart than with my heart. Can I hope that thou wouldest remember my prayers when I had almost forgotten that I had prayed? Or rather have I not cause to fear that thou rememberest my prayers too well, to punish the coldness and badness of them? Alas! are not devotions thus done, in effect, left undone? Well Jacob advised his sons, at their second going into Egypt, 'Take double money in your hands; peradventure it was an oversight.' So, Lord, I come with my second morning sacrifice: be pleased to accept it, which I desire and endeavour to present with a little better devotion than I did the former.

*   *   *

LORD, the motions of thy Holy Spirit were formerly frequent in my heart, but, alas! of late they have been great strangers. It seems they did not like their last entertainment, they are so loth to come again. I fear they were grieved, that either I heard them not attentively, or believed them not faithfully, or practised them not conscionably. If they be pleased to come again, this is all I dare promise, that they do deserve, and I do desire they should be well used. Let thy Holy Spirit be pleased not only to stand before the door and knock, but also to come in. If I do not open the door, if it were too unreasonable to request such a miracle to come in, when the doors were shut, as thou didst to the apostles. Yet let me

humbly beg of thee, that thou wouldst make the iron
gate of my heart open of its own accord (Acts xii. 10).
Then let thy Spirit be pleased to sup in my heart.   I
have given it an invitation, and I hope I shall give it
room.   But, O thou that sendest the guest, send the
meat also ; and if I be so unmannerly as not to make
the Holy Spirit welcome, O let thy effectual grace
make me to make it welcome.

*   *   *

LORD, I confess this morning I remembered my
breakfast but forgot my prayers.   And as I have returned no praise, so thou mightest justly have afforded
me no protection.   Yet thou hast carefully kept me
to the middle of the day, entrusted me with a new
debt before I have paid the old score.   It is now noon,
too late for a morning, too soon for an evening, sacrifice.   My corrupt heart prompts me to put off my
prayers till night.   But I know it too well, or rather
too ill, to trust it.   I fear, if till night I defer them,
at night I shall forget them.   Be pleased, therefore,
now to accept them.   Lord, let not a few hours the
later make a breach ; especially, seeing (being spoken
not to excuse my negligence, but to implore thy
pardon) a thousand years in thy sight are but as
yesterday.   I promise hereafter, by thy assistance, to
bring forth fruit in due season.   I am ashamed the
sun should shine on me, who now newly start in the
race of my devotions, when he, like a giant, hath run
more than half his course in the heavens.

*   *   *.

LORD, this day casually I am fallen into a bad company, and know not how I came thither, or how to

get hence. Sure I am, not my improvidence hath run me, but thy providence hath led me into this danger. I was not wandering in any base by-path, but walking in the highway of my vocation. Wherefore, Lord, thou that calledst me hither, keep me here. Stop their mouths, that they speak no blasphemy, or stop my ears, that I hear none; or open my mouth, soberly to reprove what I hear. Give me to guard myself, but, Lord, guard my guarding oi myself. Let not the smoke of their badness put out mine eyes, but the shining of mine innocency lighten theirs. Let me give physic to them, and not take infection from them. Yea, make me the better for their badness. Then shall their bad company be to me like the dirt of oysters, whose mud hath soap in it, and doth rather scour than defile.

*   *   *

LORD, often have I thought with myself, I will sin but this one sin more, and then I will repent of it, and of all the rest of my sins together. So foolish was I and ignorant. As if I should be more able to pay my debts when I owe more: or as if I should say, I will wound my friend once again, and then I will lovingly shake hands with him: but what if my friend will not shake hands with me? Besides, can one commit one sin more, and but one sin more? Grant, Lord, at this instant I may break off my badness, otherwise thou mayest justly make the last minute wherein I do sin on earth to be the last minute wherein I shall sin on earth and the first wherein thou mightest make me suffer in another place.

LORD, the preacher this day came home to my heart. A left-handed Gibeonite, with his sling (Judges x. 16), hit not the mark more sure than he my darling sins. I could find no fault with his sermon, save only that it had too much truth. But this I quarrelled at, that he went far from his text to come close to me, and so was faulty himself in telling me of my faults. Thus they will creep out at small crannies who have a mind to escape; and yet I cannot deny but that that which he spake (though nothing to that portion of Scripture which he had for his text) was according to the proportion of Scripture. And is not thy word in general the text at large of every preacher? Yea, rather I should have concluded, that if he went from his text, thy goodness sent him to meet me : for without thy guidance it had been impossible for him so truly to have traced the intricate turnings of my deceitful heart.

*   *   *

LORD, be pleased to shake my clay cottage before thou throwest it down. May it totter awhile before it doth tumble. Let me be summoned before I am surprised. Deliver me from sudden death. Not from sudden death in respect of itself; for I care not how short my passage be, so it be safe. Never any weary traveller complained that he came too soon to his journey's end. But let it not be sudden in respect of me. Make me always ready to receive death. Thus no guest comes unawares to him who keeps a constant table.

SCRIPTURE OBSERVATIONS.

LORD, in the parable of the four sorts of ground whereon the seed was sown, the last alone proved fruitful (Matt. xiii. 8). There the bad were more than the good. But amongst the servants, two improved their talents, or pounds, and one only buried them. There the good were more than the bad. Again, 'amongst the ten virgins, five were wise and five were foolish (Matt. xxv. 2). There the good and bad were equal. I see, that concerning the number of the saints in comparison to the reprobates, no certainty can be collected from these parables. Good reason, for it is not their principal purpose to meddle with that point. Grant that I may never rack a Scripture simile beyond the true intent thereof.

*   *   *

LORD, thou didst intend from all eternity to make Christ the heir of all. No danger of disinheriting him, thy only Son, and so well deserving. Yet thou sayest to him, 'Ask of me, and I will give thee the heathen for thine inheritance,' etc. This homage he must do for thy boon, to beg it. I see thy goodness delights to have thy favours sued for, expecting we should crave what thou intendest we should have; that so, though we cannot give a full price, we may take some pains for thy favours, and obtain them, though not for the merit, by the means of, our petitions.

*   *   *

LORD, I find that Ezekiel in his prophecies is styled ninety times, and more, by this appellation, 'Son of

man,' and surely not once oftener than there was
need for. For he had more visions than any one
(not to say than all) of the prophets of his time. It
was necessary, therefore, that his mortal extraction
should often be sounded in his ears, 'Son of man,' lest
his frequent conversing with visions might make him
mistake himself to be some angel. Amongst other
revelations it was therefore needful to reveal him
to himself, 'Son of man,' lest seeing many visions
might have made him blind with spiritual pride.
Lord, as thou increasest thy graces in me, and favours
on me, so with them daily increase in my soul the
monitors and remembrancers of my mortality. So
shall my soul be kept in a good temper and humble
deportment towards thee.

*   *   *

LORD, I read how Jacob (then only accompanied
with his staff) vowed at Bethel, that if thou gavest
him but bread and raiment, he would make that place
thy house. After his return, the condition on thy
side was over-performed, but the obligation on his
part wholly neglected. For when thou hadst made his
staff to swell, and to break into two bands, he, after
his return, turned purchaser (Gen. xxxiii. 19), bought
a field in Shalem, intending there to set up his rest.
But thou art pleased to be his remembrancer in a new
vision, and to spur him afresh who tired in his promise,
—'Arise, go to Bethel, and make there an altar,' etc.
Lord, if rich Jacob forgot what poor Jacob did promise,
no wonder if I be bountiful to offer thee in my affliction what I am niggardly to perform in my prosperity.
But oh! take not advantage of the forfeitures, but be

pleased to demand payment once again. Pinch me into the remembrance of my promises, that so I may re-enforce my old vows with new resolutions.

*　　*　　*

LORD, I read when our Saviour was examined in the high-priest's hall, that Peter stood without till John (being his spokesman to the maid that kept the door) procured his admission in. John meant to let him out of the cold, and not to let him into a temptation, but his courtesy in intention proved a mischief in event, and the occasion of his denying his Master. O let never my kindness concur in the remotest degree to the damage of my friend. May the chain which I sent him for an ornament never prove his fetters. But if I should be unhappy herein, I am sure thou wilt not punish my good will, but pity my ill success.

*　　*　　*

LORD, the apostle saith to the Corinthians, 'God will not suffer you to be tempted above what you are able.' But how comes he to contradict himself, by his own confession in his next Epistle, where, speaking of his own sickness, he saith, 'We were pressed out of measure, above strength'? Perchance this will be expounded by propounding another riddle of the same apostle's, who, praising Abraham, saith, 'That against hope, he believed in hope.' That is, against carnal hope, he believed in spiritual hope. So the same wedge will serve to cleave the former difficulty. Paul was pressed above his human, not above his heavenly, strength. Grant, Lord, that I may not mangle and dismember thy word, but study it entirely, comparing one place with another: for diamonds only can cut diamonds, and no such comments on the Scripture as the Scripture.

*   '   *   *

Lord, I observe that the Vulgate translation reads the apostle's precept thus : 'Give diligence to make your calling and election sure by good works.' But in our English Testament these words, 'by good works,' are left out. It grieved me at the first to see our translation defective; but it offended me afterwards to see the other redundant. For those words are not in the Greek, which is the original. And it is an ill work to put good works in, to the corruption of the Scripture. Grant, Lord, that though we leave 'good works' out in the text, we may take them in in our comment—in that exposition which our practice is to make on this precept in our lives and conversations.

*   *   *

Lord, I find the genealogy of my Saviour strangely chequered with four remarkable changes in four immediate generations.

1. 'Rehoboam begat Abiam ;' that is, a bad father begat a bad son.

2. 'Abiam begat Asa;' that is, a bad father a good son.

3. 'Asa begat Jehosaphat;' that is, a good father a good son.

4. 'Jehosaphat begat Joram;' that is, a good father a bad son.

I see, Lord, from hence, that my father's piety cannot be entailed; that is bad news for me. But I see also that actual impiety is not always hereditary; that is good news for my son.

Lord, when in my daily service I read David's psalms, give me to alter the accent of my soul according to their several subjects. In such psalms wherein he confesseth his sins, or requesteth thy pardon, or praiseth for former, or prayeth for future, favours, in all these give me to raise my soul to as high a pitch as may be. But when I come to such psalms wherein he curseth his enemies, O there let me bring my soul down to a lower note. For those words were made only to fit David's mouth. I have the like breath, but not the same spirit to pronounce them. Nor let me flatter myself that it is lawful for me, with David, to curse thine enemies, lest my deceitful heart entitle all mine enemies to be thine, and so what was religion in David prove malice in me, whilst I act revenge under the pretence of piety.

*   *   *

Lord, I read of the two witnesses, ' And when they shall have finished their testimony, the beast that ascendeth out of the bottomless pit shall make war against them, and shall overcome them, and kill them.' They could not be killed whilst they were doing, but when they had done their work; during their employment they were invincible. No better armour against the darts of death than to be busied in thy service. Why art thou so heavy, O my soul? No malice of man can antedate my end a minute whilst my Maker hath any work for me to do. And when all my daily task is ended, why should I grudge then to go to bed?

*   *   *

Lord, I read, at the transfiguration, that Peter, James, and John were admitted to behold Christ, but

Andrew was excluded. So again, at the reviving of the daughter of the ruler of the synagogue, these three were let in, and Andrew shut out. Lastly, in the agony, the aforesaid three were called to be witnesses thereof, and still Andrew left behind. Yet he was Peter's brother, and a good man, and an apostle : why did not Christ take the two brothers ? Was it not a pity to part them ? But methinks I seem more offended thereat than Andrew himself was, whom I find to express no discontent, being pleased to be accounted a loyal subject for the general, though he was no favourite in these particulars. Give me to be pleased in myself, and thankful to thee for what I am, though I be not equal to others in personal perfections, for such peculiar privileges are courtesies from thee when given, and no injuries to us when denied.

*   *   *

Lord, St. Paul teacheth the art of heavenly thrift, how to make a new sermon of an old. 'Many,' saith he, 'walk, of whom I have told you often, and now tell you weeping, that they are enemies to the cross of Christ.' Formerly he had told it with his tongue, but now with his tears ; formerly he taught it with his words, but now with weeping. Thus new affections make an old sermon new. May I not, by the same proportion, make an old prayer new ? Lord, thus long I have offered my prayer dry unto thee; now, Lord, I offer it wet. Then wilt thou own some new addition therein, when, though the sacrifice be the same, yet the dressing of it is different, being steeped in his tears who bringeth it unto thee.

LORD, I read of my Saviour, that when he was in the wilderness, 'Then the devil leaveth him, and behold angels came and ministered unto him.' A great change in a little time. No twilight betwixt night and day. No purgatory condition betwixt hell and heaven, but instantly, when out devil, in angel. Such is the case of every solitary soul. It will make company for itself. A musing mind will not stand neuter a minute, but presently side with legions of good or bad thoughts. Grant, therefore, that my soul, which ever will have some, may never have bad, company.

*　　*　　*

LORD, I read how Cushi and Ahimaaz ran a race, who first should bring tidings of victory to David. Ahimaaz, though last setting forth, came first to his journey's end; not that he had the fleeter feet, but the better brains to choose the way of most advantage. For the text saith, 'so Ahimaaz ran by the way of the plain, and overran Cushi.' Prayers made to God by saints fetch a needless compass about. That is but a rough and uneven way. Besides one steep passage therein, questionable whether it can be climbed up, and saints in heaven made sensible of what we say on earth. The way of the plain, or plain way, both shortest and surest, is, 'Call upon *me* in the time of trouble.' Such prayers (though starting last) will come first to the mark.

*　　*　　*

LORD, this morning I read a chapter in the Bible, and therein observed a memorable passage, whereof I never took notice before. Why now, and no sooner, did I see it? Formerly my eyes were as open, and the letters as legible. Is there not a thin veil laid over the word, which is rarefied by reading, and at last wholly worn away? Or was it because I came with more appetite than before? The milk was always there in the breast, but the child till now was not hungry enough to find out the teat. I see the oil of thy word will never leave increasing whilst any bring an empty barrel. The Old Testament will still be a New Testament to him who comes with a fresh desire of information.

*   *   *

LORD, at the first passover God kept touch with the Hebrews very punctually: 'At the end of the four hundred and thirty years, in the self-same day it came to pass, that all the hosts of the Lord went out of the land of Egypt:' but at the first Easter God was better than his word. Having promised that Christ should lie but three days in the grave, his fatherly affection did run to relieve him. By a charitable synecdoche two pieces of days were counted for whole ones. God did cut the work short in righteousness (Rom. ix. 28). Thus the measure of his mercy under the law was full, but it ran over in the gospel.

*   *   *

LORD, the apostle dissuadeth the Hebrews from covetousness with this argument, because God said, 'I will not leave thee nor forsake thee.' Yet I find not that God ever gave this promise to all the Jews, but he spake it only to Joshua, when first made commander against the Canaanites, which (without violence to the analogy of faith) the apostle applieth to all good men in general. Is it so that we are heirs-apparent

to all promises made to thy servants in Scripture?
Are 'the characters of grace granted to them good to
me? Then will I say with Jacob, 'I have enough.'
But because I cannot entitle myself to thy promises
to them except I imitate their piety to thee, grant I
may take as much care in following the one as comfort
in the other.

* * *

Lord, I read how Paul, writing from Rome, spake
to Philemon to prepare him a lodging, hoping to make
use thereof, yet we find not that he ever did use it,
being martyred not long after. However, he was no
loser whom thou didst lodge in a higher mansion in
heaven. Let me always be thus deceived to my
advantage. I shall have no occasion to complain,
though I never wear the new clothes fitted for me, if,
before I put them on, death clothe me with glorious
immortality.

* * *

Lord, I discover an arrant laziness in my soul; for
when I am to read a chapter in the Bible, before I
begin it I look where it endeth. And if it endeth not
on the same side, I cannot keep my hands from turning over the leaf, to measure the length thereof on the
other side; if it swells to many verses I begin to
grudge. Surely my heart is not rightly affected.
Were I truly hungry after heavenly food I would not
complain of meat. Scourge, Lord, this laziness out
of my soul; make the reading of thy word not a
penance, but a pleasure unto me; teach me that as
amongst many heaps of gold, all being equally pure,
that is the best which is the biggest, so I may esteem

that chapter in thy word the best which is the longest.

*   *   *

Lord, I find David making a syllogism, in mood and figure (Psalm lxvi.). Two propositions he perfected.

18. 'If I regard wickedness in my heart, the Lord will not hear me. 19. But verily God hath heard me, he hath attended to the voice of my prayer.'

Now I expected that David should have concluded thus :—

'Therefore I regard not wickedness in my heart.'

But far otherwise he concludes :—

20. 'Blessed be God that hath not turned away my prayer, nor his mercy from me.'

Thus David hath deceived, but not wronged me. I looked that he should have clapped the crown on his own, and he puts it on God's head. I will learn this excellent logic; for I like David's better than Aristotle's syllogisms, that whatsoever the premises be, I make God's glory the conclusion.

*   *   *

Lord, wise Agur made it his wish, 'Give me not poverty, lest I steal, and take the name of my God in vain' (Prov. xxx. 9). He saith not, lest I steal, and be caught in the manner, and then be stocked, or whipped, or branded, or forced to fourfold restitution, or put to any other shameful or painful punishment. But he saith, 'Lest I steal, and take the name of my God in vain;' that is, lest, professing to serve thee, I confute a good profession with a bad conversation. Thus thy children count sin to be the greatest smart in sin; as being more sensible of the wound they therein give to the glory of God, than of all the stripes that man may lay upon them for punishment.

* * *

LORD, I read that when my Saviour dispossessed the man's son of a devil, he enjoined the evil spirit 'To come out of him, and enter no more into him.' But I find, that when my Saviour himself was tempted of Satan, 'The devil departed from him for a season.' Retreating, as it seems, with mind to return. How came it to pass, Lord, that he who expelled him finally out of others, did not propel him so from himself? Sure it doth not follow that because he did not he could not do it; or that he was less able to help himself, because he was more charitable to relieve others. No, I see my Saviour was pleased to show himself a God in other men's matters, and but a man in such cases wherein he himself was concerned: being contented still to be tempted by Satan, that his sufferings for us might cause our conquering through him.

* * *

LORD, Jannes and Jambres (2 Tim. iii. 8), the apes of Moses and Aaron, imitated them in turning their rods into serpents; only here was the difference: Aaron's rod devoured their rods. That which was solid and substantial lasted, when that which was slight, and but seeming, vanished away. Thus an active fancy in all outward expressions may imitate a lively faith. For matter of language there is nothing what grace doth do, but wit can act. Only the difference appears in the continuance: wit is but for fits and flashes, grace holds out, and is lasting; and, good Lord, of thy goodness give it to every one that truly desires it.

HISTORICAL APPLICATIONS.

THE English ambassador, some years since, prevailed so far with the Turkish Emperor as to persuade him to hear some of our English music, from which (as from other liberal sciences) both he and his nation were naturally averse. But it happened that the musicians were so long in tuning their instruments, that the great Turk, distasting their tediousness, went away in discontent, before their music began. I am afraid that the differences and dissensions betwixt Christian churches (being so long in reconciling their discords) will breed in pagans such a disrelish of our religion, as they will not be invited to attend thereunto.

*   *   *)

A SIBYL came to Tarquinius Superbus, king of Rome, and offered to sell unto him three tomes of her oracles, but he, counting the price too high, refused to buy them. Away she went, and burnt one tome of them. Returning, she asked him, whether he would buy the two remaining at the same rate. He refused again, counting her little better than frantic. Thereupon she burns the second tome, and peremptorily asked him whether he would give the sum demanded for all the three for the one tome remaining, otherwise she would burn that also, and he would dearly repent it. Tarquin, admiring at her constant resolution, and conceiving some extraordinary worth contained therein, gave her her demand. There are three volumes of man's time—youth, man's estate, and old age—and ministers advise them to redeem this time (Ephes. v. 16). But men conceive the rate they must give to be unreasonable, because it will cost them the renouncing of their carnal delights. Hereupon one-third part of their life, youth, is consumed in the fire of wantonness. Again, ministers counsel men to redeem the remaining volumes of their life. They are but derided at for their pains. And man's estate is also cast away in the smoke of vanity. But preachers ought to press peremptorily on old people to redeem, now or never, the last volume of their life. Here is the difference: the Sibyl still demanded but the same rate for the remaining book, but aged folk (because of their custom in sinning) will find it harder and dearer to redeem this, the last volume, than if they had been chapmen for all three at the first.

* * *

In Merionethshire, in Wales, there be many mountains, whose hanging tops come so close together, that shepherds, sitting on several mountains, may audibly discourse one with another; and yet they must go many miles before their bodies can meet together, by the reason of the vast hollow valleys which are betwixt them. Our sovereign, and the members of his parliament in London, seem very near agreed in their general and public professions; both are for the Protestant religion; can they draw nearer? Both are for the privileges of parliament; can they come closer? Both are for the liberty of the subject; can they meet evener? And yet, alas, there is a great gulf and vast distance betwixt them which our sins have made, and God grant that our sorrow may seasonably make it up again.

*　　*　　*

WHEN John, king of France, had communicated the order of the knighthood of the Star to some of his guard, men of mean birth and extraction, the nobility ever after disdained to be admitted into that degree, and so that order in France was extinguished. Seeing that nowadays drinking and swearing and wantonness are grown frequent, even with base beggarly people, it is high time for men of honour, who consult with their credit, to desist from such sins. Not that I would have noblemen invent new vices to be in fashion with themselves alone, but forsake old sins, grown common with the meanest of people.

*　　*　　*

THE Roman senators conspired against Julius Cæsar to kill him. That very next morning Artemidorus, Cæsar's friend, delivered him a paper, desiring him to peruse it, wherein the whole plot was discovered: but Cæsar complimented his life away, being so taken up to return the salutations of such people as met him in the way, that he pocketed the paper, among other petitions, as unconcerned therein; and so, going to the senate-house, was slain. The world, flesh, and devil have a design for the destruction of men; we ministers bring our people a letter, God's word, wherein all the conspiracy is revealed. 'But who hath believed our_report?' Most men are so busy about worldly delights, they are not at leisure to listen to us, or read the letter; but thus, alas! run headlong to their own ruin and destruction.

*   *   *

IN the days of King Edward VI. the Lord Protector marched with a powerful army into Scotland, to demand their young queen Mary in marriage to our king, according to their promises. The Scotch, refusing to do it, were beaten by the English in Musselborough fight. One demanding of a Scottish lord, taken prisoner in the battle, 'Now, sir, how do you like our king's marriage with your queen?' 'I always,' quoth he, 'did like the marriage, but I do not like the wooing, that you should fetch a bride with fire and sword.' It is not enough for men to propound pious projects to themselves, if they go about by indirect courses to compass them. God's own work must be done by God's own ways. Otherwise we can take no comfort in obtaining the end, if we cannot justify the means used thereunto.

*   *   *

A SAGAMORE, or petty king in Virginia, guessing the greatness of other kings by his own, sent a native hither, who understood English, commanding him to score upon a long cane (given him of purpose to be his register) the number of Englishmen, that thereby his master might know the strength of this our nation. Landing at Plymouth, a populous place, and which he mistook for all England, he had no leisure to eat, for notching up the men he met. At Exeter the difficulty of his task was increased. Coming at last to London, that forest of people, he brake his

c

cane in pieces, perceiving the impossibility of his
employment. Some may conceive that they can
reckon up the sins they commit in one day. Perchance they may make hard shifts to sum up their
notorious ill deeds. More difficult it is to score up
their wicked words. But, oh, how infinite are their
idle thoughts! High time then to leave off counting,
and cry out with David, Who can tell how oft he
offendeth? Lord, cleanse me from my secret sins.

*   *   *

MARTIN DE GOLIN, master of the Teutonic Order,
was taken prisoner by the Prussians, and delivered
bound, to be beheaded. But he persuaded his executioner, who had him alone, first to take off his costly
clothes, which otherwise would be spoiled with the
sprinkling of his blood. Now the prisoner, being
partly unbound to be unclothed, and finding his
arms somewhat loosened, struck the executioner to
the ground, killed him afterwards with his own sword,
and so regained both his life and liberty. Christ hath
overcome the world, and delivered it to us to destroy
it. But we are all Achans by nature, and the Baby-
lonish garment is a bait for our covetousness. Whilst,
therefore, we seek to take plunder of this world's
wardrobe, we let go the mastery we had formerly of
it: and too often, that which Christ's passion made
our captive, our folly makes our conqueror.

*   *   *

I COULD both sigh and smile at the simplicity of a
native American, sent by a Spaniard, his master, with
a basket of figs, and a letter, wherein the figs were
mentioned, to carry them both to one of his master's

friends. By the way, this messenger eat up the figs but delivered the letter, whereby his deed was discovered, and he soundly punished. Being sent a second time on the like message, he first took the letter, which he conceived had eyes as well as a tongue, and hid it in the ground, sitting himself on the place where he put it; and then securely fell to feed on his figs, presuming that that paper, which saw nothing, could tell nothing. Then taking it again out of the ground, he delivered it to his master's friend, whereby his fault was perceived, and he worse beaten than before. Men conceive they can manage their sins with secrecy, but they carry about them a letter, or book rather, written by God's finger, their conscience bearing witness to all their actions. But sinners, being often detected and accused, hereby grow wary at last, and to prevent this speaking paper from telling any tales, do smother, stifle, and suppress it, when they go about the committing of any wickedness. Yet conscience (though buried for a time in silence) hath afterwards a resurrection, and discovers all, to their greater shame, and heavier punishment.

*   *   *

MARCUS MANLIUS deserved exceedingly well of the Roman state, having valiantly defended their capitol. But afterward, falling into disfavour with the people, he was condemned to death. However, the people would not be so unthankful as to suffer him to be executed in any place from whence the capitol might be beheld; for the prospect thereof prompted them with fresh remembrance of his former merits. At last they found a low place in the Petiline grove, by the river-gate, where no pinnacle of the capitol could be perceived, and there he was put to death. We may admire how men can find in their hearts to sin against God. For we can find no one place in the whole world which is not marked with a signal character of his mercy unto us. It was said properly of the Jews, but it is not untrue of all Christians, that they are God's vineyard. 'And God fenced it, and gathered out the stones thereof, and' planted it with the choicest vine, and built a tower in the midst thereof, and also digged a wine-press therein.' Which way can men look and not have their eyes met with the remembrance of God's favours unto them? Look about the vineyard, it is fenced; look without it, the stones are cast out; look within it, it is planted with the choicest vine; look above it, a tower is built in the midst thereof; look beneath it, a wine-press is digged. It is impossible for one to look any way, and to avoid the beholding of God's bounty. Ungrateful man! And as there is no place, so there is no time for us to sin, without being at that instant beholden to him; we owe to him that we are, even when we are rebellious against him.

*   *   *

A DUEL was to be fought, by consent of both kings, betwixt an English and a French lord. The aforesaid, John Courcy, Earl of Ulster, was chosen champion for the English, a man of great stomach and strength, but lately much weakened by long imprisonment. Wherefore, to prepare himself beforehand, the king allowed him what plenty and variety of meat he was

pleased to eat. But the monsieur (who was to encounter him) hearing what great quantity of victuals
Courcy did daily devour, and thence collecting his
unusual strength, out of fear refused to fight with
him. If by the standard of their cups, and measure
of their drinking, one might truly infer soldiers'
strength by rules of proportion, most vast and valiant
achievements may justly be expected from some
gallants of these times.

*   *   *

I HAVE heard that the brook near Lutterworth, in
Leicestershire, into which the ashes of the burnt bones
of Wickliffe were cast, never since doth drown the
meadow about it. Papists expound this to be,
because God was well pleased with the sacrifice of
the ashes of such an heretic. Protestants ascribe it
rather to proceed from the virtue of the dust of such
a reverend martyr. I see it is a case for a friend.
Such accidents signify nothing in themselves, but
according to the pleasure of interpreters. Give me
such solid reasons whereon I may rest and rely.
Solomon saith, 'The words of the wise are like nails,
fastened by the masters of the assembly.' A nail is
firm, and will hold driving in, and will hold driven in.
Send me such arguments. As for these waxen topical
devices, I shall never think worse or better of any
religion for their sake.

*   *   *

ALEXANDER the Great, when a child, was checked
by his governor, Leonidas, for being over-profuse in
spending perfumes, because on a day, being to sacrifice to the gods, he took both his hands full of

frankincense, and cast it into the fire.   But afterwards, being a man, he conquered the country of Judea (the fountain whence such spices did flow), and sent Leonidas a present of five hundred talents' weight of frankincense, to show him how his former prodigality made him thrive the better in success, and to advise him to be no more niggardly in divine service.   Thus they that sow plentifully shall reap plentifully.   I see there is no such way to have a large heart, as to have a large heart.   The free giving of the branches of our present estate to God is the readiest means to have the root increased for the future.

*   *   *

THE poets fable, that this was one of the labours imposed on Hercules, to make clean the Augean stable, or stall rather.   For therein, they said, were kept three thousand kine, and it had not been cleansed for thirty years together.   But Hercules, by letting the river Alpheus into it, did that with ease which before was conceived impossible.   This stall is the pure emblem of my impure soul, which hath been defiled with millions of sins for more than thirty years together. Oh that I might by a lively faith, and unfeigned repentance, let the stream of that fountain into my soul, ' which is opened for Judah and Jerusalem.'   It is impossible by all my pains to purge out my uncleanness, which is quickly done by the rivulet of the blood of my Saviour.

*   *   *

THE Venetians showed the treasure of their state, being in many great coffers full of gold and silver, to the Spanish ambassador. But the ambassador, peeping under the bottom of those coffers, demanded whether that their treasure did daily grow, and had a root. 'For such,' saith he, 'my master's treasure hath:' meaning both the Indies. Many men have attained to a great height of piety to be very abundant and rich therein. But all theirs is but a cistern, not fountain of grace: only God's goodness hath a spring of itself in itself.

* * *

THE Sidonian servants agreed amongst themselves to choose him to be their king who that morning should first see the sun. Whilst all others were gazing on the east, one alone looked on the west. Some admired, more mocked him, as if he looked on the feet, there to find the eye of the face. But he first of all discovered the light of the sun shining on the tops of houses. God is seen sooner, easier, clearer in his operations than in his essence. Best beheld by reflection in his creatures. 'For the invisible things of him, from the creation of the world, are clearly seen, being understood by the things that are made.'

* * *

AN Italian prince, as much delighted with the person as grieved with the prodigality of his eldest son, commanded his steward to deliver him no more money but what the young prince should tell (count) his own self. The young gallant fretted at his heart that he must buy money at so dear a rate, as to have it for telling it, but, because there was no remedy, he set himself to task, and being greatly tired with telling a small sum, he brake off in this consideration,—' Money may speedily be spent, but how tedious and troublesome is it to tell it! And by consequence, how much more difficult to get it!' Men may commit sin presently, pleasantly, with much mirth, in a moment. But O that they would but seriously consider with themselves how many their offences are, and sadly fall accounting them! And if so hard truly to sum their sins, sure harder sincerely to sorrow for them. If to get their number be so difficult, what is it to get their pardon?

*   *   *

I READ that Ægeus, the father of Theseus, hid a sword and a pair of shoes under a great stone, and left word with his wife (whom he left with child), that when the son she should bear was able to take up that stone, wield that sword, and wear those shoes, then she should send him to him, for by these signs he would own him for his own son. Christ hath left in the custody of the Church, our mother, the sword of the Spirit, and the shoes of a Christian conversation, the same which he once wore himself, and they must fit our feet; yea, and we must take up the weight of many heavy crosses before we can come at them; but when we shall appear before our heavenly Father, bringing these tokens with us, then, and not before, he will acknowledge us to be his true-born children.

MIXED CONTEMPLATIONS.

I HAVE heard some men (rather causelessly captious than judicially critical) cavil at grammarians for calling some conjunctions disjunctive, as if this were a flat contradiction. Whereas, indeed, the same particle may conjoin words, and yet disjoin the sense. But, alas! how sad is the present condition of Christians, who have a Communion disuniting. The Lord's Supper, ordained by our Saviour to conjoin our affections, hath disjoined our judgment. Yea, it is to be feared, lest our long quarrels about the manner of his presence cause the matter of his absence, for our want of charity to receive him.

* * *

I HAVE observed that children when they first put on new shoes are very curious to keep them clean. Scarce will they set their feet on the ground, for fear to dirty the soles of their shoes. Yea, rather they will wipe the leather clean with their coats; and yet perchance the next day they will trample with the same shoes in the mire, up to the ankles. Alas! children's play is our earnest. On that day wherein we receive the sacrament we are often over-precise, scrupling to say or do those things which lawfully we may. But we, who are more than curious that day, are not so much as careful the next; and too often (what shall I say) go on in sin up to the ankles, yea, our sins go over our heads (Psalm xxxviii. 4).

* * *

I KNOW some men very desirous to see the devil,

because they conceive such an apparition would be
a confirmation of their faith. For then, by the logic
of opposites, they would conclude there is a God,
because there is a devil. Thus they will not believe
there is a heaven, except hell itself will be deposed
for a witness thereof. Surely such men's wishes are
vain, and hearts are wicked; for if they will not
believe, having Moses and the prophets, and the
apostles, they will not believe (Luke xvi. 31), no,
if the devil from hell appears unto them. Such appari-
tions were never ordained by God as the means of
faith. Besides, Satan will never show himself but
to his own advantage. If as a devil, to fright them;
if as an angel of light, to flatter them; however, to
hurt them. For my part, I never desire to see him.
And O! (if it were possible) that I might never feel
him in his motions and temptations! I say, let me
never see him till the day of judgment, where he
shall stand arraigned at the bar, and God's majesty
sit judge on the bench ready to condemn him.

*   *   *

I OBSERVE that antiquaries, such as prize skill above
profit (as being rather curious than covetous), do prefer the brass coins of the Roman emperors before those
in gold and silver, because there is much falseness and
forgery daily detected (and more suspected) in gold
and silver medals, as being commonly cast and
counterfeited, whereas brass coins are presumed upon
as true and ancient, because it will not quit cost for
any to counterfeit them. Plain dealing, Lord, what
I want in wealth may I have in sincerity. I care not
how mean metal my estate be of, if my soul have the

true stamp really impressed with the unfeigned image of the King of heaven.

*   *   *

Looking on the chapel of King Henry VII., in Westminster (God grant I may once again see it, with the saint who belongs to it, our sovereign, there in a well-conditioned peace), I say, looking on the outside of the chapel, I have much admired the curious workmanship thereof. It added to the wonder, that it is so shadowed with mean houses, well-nigh on all sides, that one may almost touch it as soon as see it. Such a structure needed no base buildings about it, as foils to set it off. Rather this chapel may pass for the emblem of a great worth, living in a private way. How is he pleased with his own obscurity, whilst others of less desert make greater show? And whilst proud people stretch out their plumes in ostentation, he useth their vanity for his shelter: more pleased to have worth than to have others take notice of it.

*   *   *

The mariners at sea count it the sweetest perfume when the water in the keel of their ship doth stink. For hence they conclude that it is but little, and long since leaked in; but it is woeful with them when the water is felt before it is smelt, as fresh flowing in upon them in abundance. It is the best savour in a Christian soul when his sins are loathsome and offensive unto him. A happy token that there hath not been of late in him any insensible supply of heinous offences, because his stale sins are still his new and daily sorrow.

I HAVE sometimes considered in what troublesome case is that chamberlain in an inn, who being but one, is to give attendance to many guests. For suppose them all in one chamber, yet if one shall command him to come to the window, and the other to the table, and another to the bed, and another to the chimney, and another to come up-stairs, and another to go down-stairs, and all in the same instant, how would he be distracted to please them all. And yet such is the sad condition of my soul by nature. Not only a servant, but a slave to sin. Pride calls me to the window, gluttony to the table, wantonness to the bed, laziness to the chimney, ambition commands me to go up-stairs, and covetousness to come down. Vices, I see, are as well contrary to themselves as to virtue. Free me, Lord, from this distracted case; fetch me from being sin's servant to be thine, whose 'service is perfect freedom,' for thou art but one, and ever the same; and always enjoinest commands agreeable to themselves, thy glory, and my good.

*   *   *

I HAVE observed that towns which have been casually burnt, have been built again more beautiful than before. Mud walls, afterwards made of stone; and roofs, formerly but thatched, after advanced to be tiled. The apostle tells me That I must not think strange concerning the fiery trial which is to happen unto me (1 Peter iv. 12). May I likewise prove improved by it. Let my renewed soul, which grows out of the ashes of the old man, be a more firm fabric and strong structure; so shall affliction be my advantage.

Our Saviour saith, When thou doest alms (Matt. vi. 3), let not thy left hand know what thy right hand doeth. Yet one may generally observe that almshouses are commonly built by highway-sides, the ready road to ostentation. However, far be it from me to make bad comments on their bounty, I rather interpret it, that they place those houses so publicly, thereby, not to gain applause, but imitation. Yea, let those, who will plant pious works, have the liberty to choose their own ground. Especially in this age, wherein we are likely, neither in byways nor highways, to have any works of mercy till the whole kingdom be speedily turned into one great hospital and God's charity only able to relieve us.

* * *

Almost twenty years since I heard a profane jest, and still remember it. How many pious passages of far later date have I forgotten! It seems my soul is like a filthy pond wherein fish die soon, and frogs live long. Lord, raze this profane jest out of my memory. Leave not a letter thereof behind, lest my corruption (an apt scholar) guess it out again; and be pleased to write some pious meditation in the place thereof. And grant, Lord, for the time to come (because such bad guests are easier kept out), that I may be careful not to admit what I find so difficult to expel.

* * *

I perceive there is in the world a good nature, falsely so called, as being nothing else but a facile and flexible disposition—wax for every impression. What others are so bold to beg, they are so bashful as not to deny. Such osiers can never make beams to bear stress in church and state. If this be good nature, let me always be a clown; if this be good fellowship, let me always be a churl. Give me to set a sturdy porter before my soul, who may not equally open to every comer. I cannot conceive how he can be a friend to any, who is a friend to all, and the worst foe to himself.

*   *,   *

HA is the interjection of laughter. Ah is an interjection of sorrow. The difference betwixt them very small, as consisting only in the transposition of what is no substantial letter, but a bare aspiration. How quickly, in the age of a minute, in the very turning of a breath, is our mirth changed into mourning !

*   *   *

I HAVE a great friend whom I endeavour and desire to please, but hitherto all in vain. The more I seek the farther off I am from finding his favour. Whence comes this miscarriage? Are not my applications to man more frequent than my addresses to my Maker? Do I not love his smiles more than I fear Heaven's frowns? I confess, to my shame, that sometimes his anger hath grieved me more than my sins. Hereafter, by thy assistance, I will labour to approve my ways in God's presence; so shall I ever have, or not need, his friendship, and either please him with more ease, or displease him with less danger.

*   *   *

THIS nation is scourged with a wasting war. Our sins were ripe; God could no longer be just, if we were prosperous. Blessed be his name, that I have suffered·

my share in the calamities of my country. Had I poised myself so politically betwixt both parties that I had suffered from neither, yet could I have taken no contentment in my safe escaping. For why should I, equally engaged with others in sinning, be exempted above them from the punishment? And seeing the bitter cup, which my brethren have pledged, to pass by me, I should fear it would be filled again, and return double, for me to drink it. Yea, I should suspect that I were reserved alone for a greater shame and sorrow. It is therefore some comfort that I draw in the same yoke with my neighbours, and with them jointly bear the burden which our sins jointly brought upon us.

*   *   *

WHEN, in my private prayers, I have been to confess my bosom-sins unto God, I have been loth to speak them aloud; fearing though no man could, yet that the devil would, overhear me, and make use ot my words against me. It being probable, that when I have discovered the weakest part of my soul, he would assault me there. Yet since, I have considered, that therein I shall tell Satan no news which he knew not before. Surely I have not managed my secret sins with such privacy, but that he, from some circumstances, collected what they were. Though the fire was within, he saw some smoke without. Wherefore, for the future, I am resolved to acknowledge my darling faults, though alone, yet aloud; that the devil who rejoiced in partly knowing of my sins, may be grieved more by hearing the expression of my sorrow. As for any advantage he may make from my confession, this comforts me—God's goodness in assisting me will be above Satan's malice in assaulting me.

*   *   *

IN the midst of my morning prayers I had a good meditation, which since I have forgotten. Thus much I remember of it that it was pious in itself, but not proper for that time; for it took much from my devotion, and added nothing to my instruction; and my soul, not able to intend two things at once, abated of its fervency in praying. Thus snatching at two employments, I held neither well. Sure this meditation came not from him, who is the God of order. He used to fasten all his nails, and not to drive out one with another. If the same meditation return again, when I have leisure and room to receive it, I will say it is of his sending, who so mustereth and marshalleth all good actions, that like the soldiers in his army, mentioned by the prophet, They shall not thrust one another, they shall walk every one in his own path (Joel ii. 8).

*   *   *

WHEN I go speedily in any action, Lord, give me to call my soul to an account. It is a shrewd suspicion that my bowl runs down-hill, because it runs so fast. And, Lord, when I go in an unlawful way, start some rubs to stop me; let my foot slip or stumble: and give me the grace to understand the language of the lets thou throwest in my way. Thou hast promised, 'I will hedge up thy way;' Lord, be pleased to make the hedge high enough, and thick enough, that if I be so mad as to adventure to climb over it, I may not only soundly rake my clothes, but rend my flesh; yea, let me rather be caught, and stick in the hedge, than breaking in through it, fall on the other side into the deep ditch of eternal damnation.

* * *

Coming hastily into a chamber, I had almost thrown down a crystal hour-glass. Fear, lest I had, made me grieve as if I had broken it. But, alas! how much precious time have I cast away without any regret! The hour-glass was but crystal, each hour a pearl; that but like to be broken, this lost outright; that but casually, this done wilfully. A better hour-glass might be bought; but time lost once, lost ever. Thus we grieve more for toys than for treasure. Lord, give me an hour-glass, not to be by me, but to be in me. 'Teach me to number my days.' An hour-glass, to turn me, 'that I may apply my heart to wisdom.'

* * *

When a child I loved to look on the pictures in the *Book of Martyrs.* I thought that there the martyrs at the stake seemed like the three children in the fiery furnace, ever since I had known them there, not one hair more of their head was burnt, nor any smell of the fire singeing of their clothes (Dan. iii. 27). This made me think martyrdom was nothing. But, oh! though the lion be painted fiercer than he is, the fire is far fiercer than it is painted. Thus it is easy for one to endure an affliction, as he limns it out in his own fancy, and represents it to himself but in a bare speculation. But when it is brought indeed, and laid home to us, there must be a man, yea, there must be God to assist the man to undergo it.

TRAVELLING on the plain (which notwithstanding hath its risings and fallings), I discovered Salisbury steeple many miles off. Coming to a declivity, I lost the sight thereof; but climbing up to the next hill, the steeple grew out of the ground again. Yea, I often found it, and lost it, till at last I came safely to it, and took my lodging near it. It fareth thus with us whilst we are wayfaring to heaven; mounted on the Pisgah-top of some good meditation, we get a glimpse of our celestial Canaan; but when either on the flat of an ordinary temper, or in the fall of some extraordinary temptation, we lose the view thereof. Thus in the sight of our soul heaven is discovered, covered, and recovered; till, though late, at last, though slowly, surely, we arrive at the haven of our happiness.

*   *   *

LORD, I find myself in the latitude of a fever. I am neither well nor ill. Not so well that I have any mind to be merry with my friends, nor so ill that my friends have any cause to condole with me. I am a probationer in point of my health. As I shall behave myself, so I may be either expelled out of it, or admitted into it. Lord, let my distemper stop here, and go no farther. Shoot thy murdering pieces against that clay castle which surrendereth itself at thy first summons. O spare me a little, that I may recover my strength. I beg not to be forgiven, but to be forborne my debt to nature. And I only do crave time for a while, till I be better fitted and furnished to pay it.

*   *   *

IT seemed strange to me when I was told that

Aqua vitæ, which restores life to others, should itself be made of the droppings of dead beer. And that strong waters should be extracted out of the dregs (almost) of small beer. Surely many other excellent ingredients must concur, and much art must be used in the distillation. Despair not, then, O my soul! no extraction is impossible where the chemist is infinite. He that is all in all can produce anything out of anything. And he can make my soul, which by nature is 'settled on her lees,' and dead in sin, to be quickened by the infusion of his grace, and purified into a pious disposition.

*   *   *

How easy is pen and paper piety, for one to write religiously? I will not say it costeth nothing, but it is far cheaper to work one's head than one's heart to goodness. Some, perchance, may guess me to be good by my writings, and so I shall deceive my reader. But if I do not desire to be good, I most of all deceive myself. I can make an hundred meditations sooner than subdue the least sin in my soul. Yea, I was once in the mind never to write more, for fear lest my writings at the last day prove records against me. And yet why should I not write? that by reading my own book, the disproportion betwixt my lines and my life may make me blush myself (if not into goodness) into less badness than I would do otherwise. That so my writings may condemn me, and make me to condemn myself, that so God may be moved to acquit me.

PERSONAL MEDITATIONS.

Curiosity curbed.—Often have I thought with myself what disease I would be best contented to die of. None please me. The stone, or the colic, terrible as expected, intolerable when felt. The palsy is death before death. The consumption a flattering disease, cozening men into hope of long life at the last gasp. Some sicknesses besot, other enrage men, some are too swift, and others too slow.

If I could as easily decline diseases as I could dislike them, I should be immortal. But away with these thoughts. The mark must not choose what arrow shall be shot against it. What God sends I must receive. May I not be so curious to know what weapon shall wound me, as careful to provide the plaster of patience against it. Only thus much in general: commonly that sickness seizeth on men which they least suspect. He that expects to be drowned with a dropsy may be burnt with a fever; and she that fears to be swollen with a tympany may be shrivelled with a consumption.

Deceived, not hurt.—Hearing a passing bell, I prayed that the sick man might have, through Christ, a safe voyage to his long home. Afterwards I understood that the party was dead some hours before; and it seems in some places of London the tolling of the bell is but a preface of course to the ringing it out.

Bells better silent than thus telling lies. What is

this but giving a false alarm to men's devotions, to make them to be ready armed with their prayers for the assistance of such who have already fought the good fight, yea, and gotten the conquest? Not to say that men's charity herein may be suspected of superstition in praying for the dead.

However, my heart thus poured out was not spilt on the ground. My prayers, too late to do him good, came soon enough to speak my good will. What I freely tendered, God fairly took, according to the integrity of my intention. The party, I hope, is in Abraham's, and my prayers I am sure are returned into my own bosom.

Nor full, nor fasting.—Living in a country village where a burial was a rarity, I never thought of death, it was so seldom presented unto me. Coming to London, where there is plenty of funerals (so that coffins crowd one another, and corpses in the grave jostle for elbow-room), I slight and neglect death, because grown an object so constant and common.

How foul is my stomach to turn all food into bad humours! Funerals, neither few nor frequent, work effectually upon me. London is a library of mortality. Volumes of all sorts and sizes; rich, poor, infants, children, youth, men, old men, daily die. I see there is more required to make a good scholar than only the having of many books. Lord, be thou my schoolmaster, and 'teach me to number my days, that I may apply my heart unto wisdom.'

Strange and True.—I read, in the Revelation, of a beast, one of whose 'heads was as it were wounded to death.' I expected in the next verse that the beast

should die, as the most probable cosequence, considering :

1. It was not a scratch, but a wound ;

2. Not a wound in a fleshy part, or out-limbs of
the body, but in the very head, the throne of reason ;

3. No light wound, but in outward apparition
(having no other probe but St. John's eyes to search
it), it seemed deadly.

But mark what immediately follows : ' And his
deadly wound was healed.' Who would have suspected this inference from these premises. But is not
this the lively emblem of my natural corruption?
Sometimes I conceive that by God's grace I have
conquered and killed, subdued and slain, maimed and
mortified the deeds of the flesh ; never more shall I
be molested or buffeted with such a bosom sin : when
alas! by the next return, the news is, it is revived,
and recovered. Thus tenches, though grievously
gashed, presently plaster themselves whole by that
slimy and unctuous humour they have in them ; and
thus the inherent balsam of badness quickly cures my
corruption, not a scar to be seen. I perceive I shall
never finally kill it till, first, I be dead myself.

Blushing to be blushed for.—A person of great
quality was pleased to lodge a night in my house. I
durst not invite him to my family prayer, and therefore
for that time omitted it : thereby making a breach in
a good custom, and giving Satan advantage to assault
it. Yea, the loosening of such a link might have en-
dangered the scattering of the chain.

Bold bashfulness, which durst offend God, whilst it
did fear man! Especially considering, that though

my guest was never so high, yet, by the laws of hospitality, I was above him whilst under my roof. Hereafter, whosoever cometh within the doors shall be requested to come within the discipline of my house; if accepting my homely diet, he will not refuse my home devotion; and sitting at my table, will be intreated to kneel down by it.

A lash for laziness.—Shameful my sloth, that have deferred my night prayer till I am in bed. This lying along is an improper posture for piety. Indeed, there is no contrivance of our body, but some good man in Scripture hath handselled it with prayer. The publican standing, Job sitting, Hezekiah lying on his bed, Elijah with his face between his legs. But of all gestures give me St. Paul's, 'For this cause I bow my knees to the Father of my Lord Jesus Christ.' Knees, when they may, then they must, be bended.

I have read a copy of a grant of liberty from Queen Mary to Henry Ratcliff, Earl of Sussex, giving him leave to wear a cap, or coif, in her Majesty's presence, counted a great favour because of his infirmity. I know in case of necessity God would graciously accept my devotion bound down in a sick dressing, but now whilst I am in perfect health it is inexcusable. Christ commanded some to take up their bed, in token of their full recovery: my laziness may suspect, lest my bed thus taking me up, prove a presage of my ensuing sickness. But may God pardon my idleness this once, I will not again offend in the same kind by his grace hereafter.

Root, branch, and fruit.—A poor man of Seville, in Spain, having a fair and fruitful pear-tree, one of the fathers of the Inquisition desired (such tyrants' requests are commands) some of the fruit thereof. The poor man, not out of gladness to gratify, but fear to offend, as if it were a sin for him to have better fruit than his betters (suspecting on his denial the tree might be made his own rod, if not his gallows), plucked up tree, roots and all, and gave it unto him.

Allured with love to God, and advised by mine own advantage, what he was frighted to do I will freely perform. God calleth on me to present him with 'fruits meet for repentance.' Yea, let him take all; soul and body, powers and parts, faculties and members of both, I offer a sacrifice unto himself. Good reason, for indeed the tree was his, before it was mine, and I give him of his own.

Besides, it was doubtful whether the poor man's material tree, being removed, would grow again. Some plants, transplanted (especially when old) become sullen, and do not enjoy themselves in a soil wherewith they were unacquainted. But sure I am, when I have given myself to God, the moving of my soul shall be the mending of it, he will so dress, so prune, and purge me, that I shall bring forth most fruit in my age.

God speed the plough.—I saw in seed-time a husbandman at plough in a very raining day. Asking him the reason why he would not rather leave off than labour in such foul weather, his answer was returned me in their country rhythm :—

> ' Sow beans in the mud,
> And they'll come up like a wood.'

This could not but remind me of David's expression, ' They that sow in tears, shall reap in joy. He that goeth forth and weepeth, bearing precious seed, shall doubtless come again with rejoicing, bringing his sheaves with him' (Psalm cxxvi. 5, 6).

These last five years have been a wet and woeful seed-time to me, and many of my afflicted brethren. Little hope have we, as yet, to come again to our own homes, and in a literal sense, now to bring our sheaves, which we see others daily to carry away on their shoulders. But if we shall not share in the former or latter harvest here on earth, the third and last in heaven we hope undoubtedly to receive.

Cras, cras.—Great was the abundance and boldness of the frogs in Egypt, which went up and came into their bed-chambers, and beds, and kneading-troughs, and very ovens. Strange that those fen-dwellers should approach the fiery region; but stranger, that Pharaoh should be so backward to have them removed, and being demanded of Moses when he would have them sent away, answered, To-morrow. He could be content with their company one night, at bed and at board, loth, belike, to acknowledge either God's justice in sending, or power in remanding them, but still hoping that they casually came, and might casually depart (Exod. viii. 3).

Leave I any longer to wonder at Pharaoh, and even admire at myself. What are my sins but so many toads, spitting of venom and spawning of poison, croaking in my judgment, creeping into my will, and crawling into my affections! This I see, and suffer, and say with Pharaoh, To-morrow, to-morrow will I amend. Thus, as the Hebrew tongue hath no proper present tense, but two future tenses, so all the performances of my reformation are only in promises for the time to come. Grant, Lord, I may seasonably drown this Pharaoh-like procrastination in the sea of repentance, lest it drown me in the pit of perdition.

Green when grey.—In September I saw a tree bearing roses, whilst others of the same kind round about it were barren. Demanding the cause of the gardener why that tree was an exception from the rule of the rest, this reason was rendered; because that alone being clipped close in May, was then hindered to spring and sprout, and therefore took this advantage by itself to bud in autumn.

Lord, if I were curbed and snipped in my younger years, by fear of my parents, from those vicious excrescences to which that age was subject, give me to have a godly jealousy over my heart, suspecting an autumn-spring, lest corrupt nature (which without thy restraining grace will have a vent) break forth in my reduced years into youthful vanities.

Miserere.—There goes a tradition of Ovid, that famous poet (receiving some countenance from his own confession), that when his father was about to beat him for following the pleasant but profitless study of poetry, he, under correction, promised his father never to make a verse, and made a verse in his very promise. Probably the same in sense, but certainly more elegant for composure, than this verse which common credulity hath taken up.

'*Parce precor, genitor, posthac non versificabo.*'
    'Father, on me pity take,
      Verses I no more will make.'

When I so solemnly promise my heavenly Father

to sin no more, I sin in my very promise. My weak prayers, made to procure my pardon, increase my guiltiness. O the dulness and deadness of my heart therein! I say my prayers, as the Jews eat the pass-over, in haste. And whereas in bodily actions motion is the cause of heat, clean contrary, the more speed I make in my prayers, the colder I am in my devotion.

What helps not, hurts.—A vain thought arose in my heart; instantly my corruption retains itself to be the advocate for it, pleading that the worst that could be said against it was this, that it was a vain thought.

And is not this the best that can be said for it? Remember, O my soul, the fig-tree was charged, not with bearing noxious, but no fruit. Yea, the barren fig-tree bare the fruit of annoyance. 'Cut it down, why cumbereth it the ground?' Vain thoughts do this ill in my heart, that they do no good.

Besides, the fig-tree pestered but one part of the garden; good grapes might grow, at the same time, in other places of the vineyard. But seeing my soul is so intent on its object, that it cannot attend two things at once, one tree for the time being is all my vineyard. A vain thought engrosseth all the ground of my heart; till that be rooted out no good meditation can grow with it or by it.

Always seen, never minded.—In the most healthful times, two hundred, and upwards, was the constant weekly tribute payed to mortality in London. A large bill, but it must be discharged. Can one city spend according to this weekly rate, and be not bank-

rupt of people? at leastwise, must not my shot be
called for, to make up the reckoning?

When only seven young men, and those chosen by
lot, were but yearly taken out of Athens, to be devoured
by the monster Minotaur, the whole city was in a constant fright, children for themselves, and parents for
their children. Yea, their escaping of the first was
but an introduction to the next year's lottery.

Were the dwellers and lodgers in London weekly to
cast lots who should make up this two hundred, how
would every one be affrighted? Now none regard
it. My security concludes the aforesaid number will
amount of infants and old folk. Few men of middle
age, and amongst them surely not myself. But, oh!
is not this putting the evil day far from me, the ready
way to bring it the nearest to me? The lot is weekly
drawn, though not by me, for me; I am therefore
concerned seriously to provide, lest that death's prize
prove my blank.

Not whence, but whither.—Finding a bad
thought in my heart, I disputed in myself the cause
thereof, whether it proceeded from the devil, or mine
own corruption, examining it by those signs divines
in this case recommended.

1. Whether it came in incoherently, or by depend-
ence on some object presented to my senses.

2. Whether the thought was at full age at the first
instant, or, infant-like, grew greater by degrees.

3. Whether out or in the road of my natural inclination.

But hath not this inquiry more of curiosity than
religion? Hereafter derive not the pedigree, but make

the mittimus of such malefactors. Suppose a con-
federacy betwixt thieves without and false servants
within, to assault and wound the master of a family ;
thus wounded, would he discuss from which of them his
hurts proceeded? No, surely, but speedily send for a
surgeon, before he bleed to death. I will no more put
it to the question whence my bad thoughts come, but
whither I shall send them, lest this curious controversy
insensibly betray me into a consent unto them.

Storm, steer on.—The mariners sailing with St.
Paul bare up bravely against the tempest, whilst either
art or industry could befriend them. Finding both to
fail, and that they could not any longer ' bear up into
the wind,' they even let their ship drive (Acts xxvii. 15).
I have endeavoured in these distemperate times to hold
up my spirits, and to steer them steadily. A happy
peace here was the port whereat I desired to arrive.
Now, alas! the storm grows too sturdy for the pilot.
Hereafter all the skill I will use is no skill at all, but
even let my ship sail whither the winds send it.

Noah's ark was bound for no other port but preservation for the present (that ship being all the har-
bour), not intending to find land, but to float on water.
May my soul, though not sailing to the desired haven,
only be kept from sinking in sorrow. This comforts
me, that the most weather-beaten vessel cannot properly be seized on for a wreck which hath any quick
cattle remaining there. My spirits are not as yet forfeited to despair, having one lively spark of hope in
my heart, because God is even where he was before.

Wit outwitted.—Joab chid the man (unknown
in Scripture by his name, well known for his wisdom)

for not killing Absalom when he saw him hanged in the tree, promising him for his pains ten shekels and a girdle. But the man (having the king's command to the contrary) refused his proffer. Well he knew that politic statesman would have dangerous designs fetched out of the fire, but with other men's fingers. His girdle promised, might in payment prove an halter. Yea, he added moreover, that had he killed Absalom, Joab himself would have set himself against him (2 Sam. xviii. 13).

Satan daily solicits me to sin (point-blank against God's word), baiting me with proffers best pleasing my corruption. If I consent, he who last tempted first accuseth me. The fawning spaniel turns a fierce lion, and roareth out my faults in the ears of heaven. Grant, Lord, when Satan shall next serve me as Joab did this nameless Israelite, I may serve him as the nameless Israelite did Joab, flatly refusing his deceitful tenders.

Hereafter.—David fasted and prayed for his sick son, that his life might be prolonged. But when he was dead, this consideration comforted him: 'I shall go to him, but he shall not return to me" (2 Sam. xii. 23).

Peace did long lie languishing in this land. No small contentment that, to my poor power, I have prayed and preached for the preservation thereof. Seeing, since it is departed, this supports my soul, having little hope that peace here should return to me, I have some assurance that I shall go to peace hereafter.

Bad at best.—Lord, how come wicked thoughts

to perplex me in my prayers, when I desire and endeavour only to attend thy service? Now I perceive the cause thereof; at other times I have willingly entertained them, and now they entertain themselves against my will. I acknowledge thy justice, that what formerly I have invited, now I cannot expel. Give me hereafter always to bolt out such ill guests. The best way to be rid of such bad thoughts in my prayers is not to receive them out of my prayers.

Compendium dispendium.—Pope Boniface IX., at the end of each hundred years, appointed a jubilee at Rome, wherein people, bringing themselves and money thither, had pardon for their sins.

But centenary years returned but seldom. Popes were old before, and covetous when they came to their place. Few had the happiness to fill their coffers with jubilee coin. Hereupon Clement VI. reduced it to every three-and-thirtieth, Paul II. and Sixtus IV. to every twenty-fifth year.

Yea, an agitation is reported in the conclave, to bring down jubilees to fifteen, twelve, or ten years, had not some cardinals (whose policy was above their covetousness) opposed it.

I serve my prayers as they their jubilees. Perchance they may extend to a quarter of an hour, when poured out at large. But some days I begrudge this time as too much, and omit the preface of my prayer, with some passages conceived less material, and run two or three petitions into one, so contracting them to half a quarter of an hour.

Not long after, this also seems too long. I decontract and abridge the abridgment of my prayers. Yea,

(be it confessed to my shame and sorrow, that hereafter I may amend it) too often I shrink my prayers
to a minute, to a moment, to a 'Lord have mercy
upon me.'

SCRIPTURE OBSERVATIONS.

The vicious mean.—Zophar, the Naamathite,
mentioneth a sort of men in whose mouths wickedness
is sweet. 'They hide it under their tongues, they
spare it, and forsake it not, but keep it still in their
mouths' (Job xx. 12, 13.) This furnisheth me with
a tripartite division of men in the world.

The first and best are those who spit sin out,
loathing it in their judgments, and leaving it in their
practice.

The second sort, notoriously wicked, who swallow
sin down, actually and openly committing it.

The third endeavouring an expedient between heaven and hell, neither do not deny their lusts, neither
spitting them out, nor swallowing them down, but
rolling them under their tongues, epicurising thereon
in their filthy fancies and obscene speculations.

If God at the last day of judgment hath three
hands, a right for the sheep, a left for the goats, the
middle is most proper for these third sort of men.
But both these latter kinds of sinners shall be confounded together, the rather because a sin thus rolled
becomes so soft and supple, and the throat is so short
and slippery a passage, that insensibly it may slide
down from the mouth into the stomach; and contem-

plative wantonness quickly turns into practical un-cleanness.

Store no sore.—Job had a custom to offer burnt-offerings according to the number of his sons, for, he said, 'It may be that my sons in their feasting have sinned, and cursed God in their hearts.' It may be, not it must be, he was not certain, but suspected it. But now, what if his sons had not sinned? Was Job's labour lost, and his sacrifice of none effect? Oh, no! only their property was altered. In case his sons were found faulty, his sacrifices for them were propitiatory, and through Christ obtained their pardon; in case they were innocent, his offerings were eucharistical, returning thanks to God's restraining grace, for keeping his sons from such sins, which otherwise they would have committed.

I see in all doubtful matters of devotion, it is wisest to be on the surest side, better both lock and bolt and bar it, than leave the least door of danger open. Hast thou done what is disputable whether it be well done? Is it a measuring cast whether it be lawful or no? So that thy conscience may seem in a manner to stand neuter, sue a conditional pardon out of the court of heaven, the rather because our self-love is more prone to flatter than our godly jealousy to suspect ourselves without a cause; with such humility heaven is well pleased. For suppose thyself over-cautious, needing no forgiveness in that particular, God will interpret the pardon thou prayest for to be the praises presented unto him.

Line on line.—Moses, in God's name, did counsel Joshua (Deuteronomy xxxi. 23), 'Be strong, and of a

D

good courage, for thou shalt bring the children of
Israel into the land which I sware unto them.' God
immediately did command him (Joshua i. 6), 'Be
strong and of a good courage;' and again (verse 7),
'Only be thou strong and very courageous;' and
again (verse 9), 'Have I not commanded thee? Be
strong and of a good courage, be not afraid, neither
be thou dismayed.' Lastly, the Reubenites and Gadites
heartily desired him (verse 28), 'Only be strong, and
of a good courage.'

Was Joshua a dunce or a coward? Did his wit or
his valour want an edge, that the same precept must
so often be pressed upon him? No doubt neither, but
God saw it needful that Joshua should have courage
of proof, who was to encounter both the froward Jew
and the fierce Canaanite.

Though metal on metal, colour on colour, be false
heraldry; line on line, precept on precept is true divinity.

Be not therefore offended, O my soul, if the same
doctrine be often delivered unto thee by different
preachers, if the same precept (like the sword in
Paradise which turned every way) doth hunt and
haunt thee, tracing thee which way soever thou
turnest; rather conclude that thou art deeply concerned in the practice thereof which God has thought
fit should be so frequently inculcated into thee.

O! the depth.—Had I beheld Sodom in the beauty
thereof, and had the angel told me that the same
should be suddenly destroyed by a merciless element,
I should certainly have concluded that Sodom should
have been drowned—led thereunto by these considerations:

1. It was situated in the plain of Jordan, a flat, low, level country;

2. It was well watered everywhere; and where always there is water enough, there may sometimes be too much;

3. Jordan had a quality in the first month to overflow all his banks.

But no drop of moisture is spilt on Sodom; it is burnt to ashes. How wide are our conjectures, when they guess at God's judgments! How far are his ways above our apprehension! Especially when wicked men with the Sodomites wander in strange sins, out of the road of common corruption, God meets them with strange punishments, out of the reach of common conception, not coming within the compass of a rational suspicion.

Self, self-hurter.—When God at the first day of judgment arraigned Eve, she transferred her fault on the serpent which beguiled her. This was one of the first-fruits of our depraved nature. But, ever after, regenerate men in Scripture, making the confession of their sins (whereof many precedents), cast all the fault on themselves alone; yea, David, when he numbered the people, though it be expressed that Satan provoked him thereunto, and though David probably might be sensible of his temptation, yet he never accused the devil, but derived all the guilt on himself—'I it is that have sinned' (1 Chron. xxi. 17) : good reason, for Satan hath no impulsive power, he may strike fire till he be weary (if his malice can be weary); except man's corruption brings the tinder, the match cannot be lighted. Away, then, with the plea of course,—' The devil owed me a shame.' Owe thee he might, but pay thee he could not, unless thou wert as willing to take his black money as he to tender it.

Gad, Behold a troop cometh.—The Amalekite who brought the tidings to David began with truth, rightly reporting the overthrow of the Israelites (2 Sam. i.). Cheaters must get some credit before they can cozen, and all falsehood, if not founded in some truth, would not be fixed in any belief.

But proceeding, he told six lies successively:

1. That Saul called him;
2. That he came at his call;
3. That Saul demanded who he was;
4. That he returned his answer;
5. That Saul commanded him to kill him;
6. That he killed him accordingly.

A wilful falsehood told is a cripple not able to stand by itself without some one to support it. It is easy to tell a lie, hard to tell but a lie.

Lord, if I be so unhappy to relate a falsehood, give me to recall it or repent of it. It is said of the pismires, that to prevent the growing (and so the corrupting) of that corn which they hoard up for their winter provision, they bite off both the ends thereof, wherein the generating power of the grain doth consist. When I have committed a sin, O let me so order it that I may destroy the procreation thereof, and, by a true sorrow, condemn it to a blessed barrenness.

Out means, in miracles.—When the angel brought St. Peter out of prison, the iron gate opened of its own accord. But coming to the house of Mary, the mother of John and Mark, he was feign to stand before the door, and knock. When iron gave obedience, how can wood make opposition?

The answer easy. There was no man to open the iron gate, but a portress was provided, of course, to unlock the door. God would not therefore show his finger where men's hands were appointed to do the work. Heaven will not super-institute a miracle, where ordinary means were formerly in peaceable possession. But if they either depart or resign (ingenuously confessing their insufficiency), there miracles succeed in their vacancy.

No stool of wickedness.—Sometimes I have disputed with myself which of the two were most guilty: David, who said in haste 'all men are liars,' or that wicked man who sat and spake against his brother, and slandered his own mother's son (Psalm l. 20).

David seems the greater offender; for mankind might have an action of defamation against him, yea, he might justly be challenged for giving all men the lie. But mark, David was in haste, he spake it *in transitu*, when he was passing, or rather posting by, or if you please, not David, but David's haste rashly vented the word. Whereas the other sat, a sad, solemn, serious, premeditate, deliberate posture: his malice had a full blow with a steady hand, at the credit of his brother. Not to say that *sat* carries with it the countenance of a judicial proceeding, as if he made a session or bench-business thereof, as well condemning as accusing unjustly.

Lord, pardon my cursory, and preserve me from sedentary sins. If in haste or heat of passion I wrong any, give me at leisure to ask thee and them forgiveness. But oh, let me not sit by it, studiously to plot or project mischief to any out of malice prepense. To shed blood in cool blood, is blood with a witness.

The best bed-maker.—When a good man is ill at ease, God promiseth to make all his bed in his sickness (Psalm xli. 3). Pillow, bolster, head, feet, sides, *all* his bed. Surely that God who made him knows so well his measure and temper, as to make his bed to please him. Herein his art is excellent, not fitting the bed to the person, but the person to the bed, infusing patience into him.

But oh, how shall God make my bed, who have no bed of mine own to make? Thou fool, he can make thy not having a bed to be a bed unto thee. When Jacob slept on the ground, who would not have had his hard lodging, therewithal to have his heavenly dream? Yea, the poor woman in Jersey, which in the reign of Queen Mary was delivered of a child as she was to be burnt at the stake, may be said to be brought to bed in the fire. Why not? If God's justice threatened to cast Jezebel into a bed of fire (Rev. ii. 22), why might not his mercy make the very flames a soft bed to that his patient martyr?

Too late, too late.—The elder brother laid a sharp and true charge against his brother prodigal for his riot and luxury. This nothing affected his father, the mirth, meat, music at the feast, was notwithstanding no whit abated. Why so? because the elder brother was the younger in this respect, and came too late.

The other had got the speed of him, having first accused himself (nine verses before), and already obtained his pardon.

Satan (to give him his due) is my brother, and my elder by creation. Sure I am, he will be my grievous accuser. I will endeavour to prevent him, first condemning myself to God my Father. So shall I have an act of indemnity before he can enter his action against me.

Lawful stealth.—I find two (husband and wife) both stealing, and but one of them guilty of felony. 'And Rachel had stolen the images that were her father's, and Jacob stole away, unawares to Laban the Syrian' (Gen. xxxi. 19, 20). In the former a complication of theft, lying, sacrilege, and idolatry; in the latter no sin at all. For what our conscience tells us is lawful, and our discretion dangerous, it is both conscience and discretion to do it with all possible secrecy. It was as lawful for Jacob in that case privately to steal away, as it is for that man who finds the sunshine too hot for him to walk in the shade.

God keep us from the guilt of Rachel's stealth. But for Jacob's stealing away, one may confess the fact, but deny the fault therein. Some are said to have gotten their life for a prey; if any, in that sense, have preyed on (or, if you will, plundered) their own liberty, stealing away from the place where they conceived themselves in danger, none can justly condemn them.

Text improved.—I heard a preacher take for his text, 'Am not I thine ass, upon which thou hast ridden ever since I was thine unto this day? was I ever wont to do so unto thee ? ' (Numb. xxii. 30). I wondered what he would make thereof, fearing he would starve his auditors for want of matter. But hence he observed:

1. The silliest and simplest, being wronged, may justly speak in their own defence ;·

2. Worst men have a good title to their own goods. Balaam a sorcerer, yet the ass confesseth twice he was his ;

3. They who have done many good offices, and fail in one, are often not only unrewarded for former service, but punished for that one offence ;

4. When the creatures, formerly officious to serve us, start from their wonted obedience (as the earth to become barren, and air pestilential), man ought to reflect on his own sin as the sole cause thereof.

How fruitful are the seeming barren places of Scripture. Bad ploughmen, which make balks of such ground. Wheresoever the surface of God's word doth not laugh and sing with corn, there the heart thereof within is merry with mines, affording, where not plain matter, hidden mysteries.

The Royal bearing.—God is said to have brought the Israelites out of Egypt on eagles' wings (Exod. xix. 4). Now eagles, when removing their young ones, have a different posture from other fowl proper to themselves (fit it is that there should be a distinction betwixt sovereign and subject), carrying their prey in their talons, but young ones on their backs, so interposing their whole bodies betwixt them and harm. The old eagle's body is the young eagle's shield, and must be shot through before her young ones can be hurt.

Thus God, in saving the Jews, put himself betwixt them and danger. Surely God, so loving under the law, is no less gracious in the gospel. Our souls are better secured, not only above his wings, but in his body. 'Your life is hid with Christ in God.' No fear then of harm; God first must be pierced before we can be prejudiced.

None to him.—It is said of our Saviour, his 'fan is in his hand.' How well it fits him, and he it! Could Satan's clutches snatch the fan, what work would he make! He would fan as he doth winnow, in a tempest, yea, in a whirlwind, and blow the best away. Had man the fan in his hand, especially in these distracted times, out goes for chaff all opposite to the opinions of his party. Seeming sanctity will carry it away from such, who, with true but weak grace, have ill natures and eminent corruptions.

There is a kind of darnel, called *Lolium murium*, because so counterfeiting corn, that even the mice themselves (experience should make them good tasters) are sometimes deceived therewith. Hypocrites, in like manner, so act holiness that they pass for saints before men, whose censures often barn up the chaff, and burn up the grain.

Well then! Christ for my share. The fan is in so good a hand, it cannot be mended. Only his hand, who knows hearts, is proper for that employment.

Humility.—It is a strange passage (Rev. vii. 13, 14),—'And one of the elders answered, saying unto me, What are these which are arrayed in white robes? and whence came they? And I said unto him, Sir, thou knowest. And he said to me, These arc they which came out of great tribulation,' etc.

How comes the elder, when asking a question, to be said to answer? On good reason: for his *quære* in effect was a resolution. He asked St. John, not because he thought he could, but knew he could not answer, that John's ingenuous confession of his ignorance might invite the elder to inform him.

As his question is called an answer, so God's commands are grants. When he enjoins us, ' Repent, believe,' it is only to draw from us a free acknowledgment of our impotency to perform his commands. This confession being made by us, what he enjoins he will enable us to do. Man's owning his weakness is the only stock for God thereon to graft the grace of his assistance.

MEDITATIONS ON ALL KINDS OF PRAYERS.

Newly awaked.—By the Levitical law the firstling of every clean creature was holy to God. By the moral analogy thereof, this first glance of mine eyes is due to him. By the custom of this kingdom there accrueth to the landlord a fine and heriot from his tenant taking a farther estate in his lease. I hold from God this clay cottage of my body—a homely tenement, but may I in some measure be assured of a better before outed of this. Now being raised from last night's sleep, I may seem to renew a life. What shall I pay to my landlord? Even the best quick creature which is to be found on my barren copyhold, namely, ' the calves of my lips,' praising him for his protection over me. More he doth not ask, less I cannot give; yea, such is his goodness, and my weakness, that before I can give him thanks he giveth me to be thankful.

Family prayer.—Long have I searched the Scriptures to find a positive precept enjoining, or precedent observing, daily prayer in a family, yet hitherto have found none proper for my purpose. Indeed, I read that there was a yearly sacrifice offered at Bethlehem for the family of Jesse; but if hence we should infer household holy duties, others would conclude they should only be annual. And whereas it is said, Pour out thine indignation on the heathen, and on the families which have not called on thy name; the word taken there in a large acceptation, reproveth rather the want of national than domestic service of God (1 Sam. xx. 29; Jer. x. 25).

But let not profaneness improve itself, or censure family prayer for will-worship, as wanting a warrant in God's word. For where God enjoineth a general duty, as to serve and fear Him, there, all particular means (whereof prayer a principal) tending thereunto are commanded. And surely the pious households of Abraham, Joshua, and Cornelius had some holy exercises to themselves, as broader than their personal devotion, so narrower than the public service, just adequate to their own private family.

Self without other Self.—Some loving wife may perchance be (though not angry with) grieved at her husband for excluding her from his private prayers, thus thinking with herself—'Must I be discommuned from my husband's devotions? what? several closet-

chapels for those of the same bed and board? Are
not our credits embarked in the same bottom, so that
they sink or swim together? May I not be admitted
an auditor at his petitions, were it only to say Amen
thereunto?'

But let such a one seriously consider what the
prophet saith,—'The family of the house of David
apart, and their wives apart; the family of the house
of Nathan apart, and their wives apart' (Zech. xii. 12).
Personal private faults must be privately confessed.
It is not meet she should know all the bosom sins of
him in whose bosom she lieth. Perchance being now
offended for not hearing her husband's prayers, she
would be more offended if she heard them. Nor hath
she just cause to complain, seeing herein Nathan's
wife is equal with Nathan himself; what liberty she
alloweth is allowed her, and may, as well as her
husband, claim the privilege privately and apart, to
pour forth her soul unto God in her daily devotions.
Yet man and wife, at other times, ought to communicate in their prayers, all others excluded.

Groans.—How comes it to pass that groans made
in men by God's spirit cannot be uttered? I find two
reasons thereof. First, because those groans are so
low and little, so faint, frail, and feeble, so next to
nothing; these still-born babes only breathe without
crying.

Secondly, because so much diversity, yea, con-
trariety of passion, is crowded within the compass of
a groan, they are stayed from being expressive, and
the groans become unutterable.

How happy is their condition who have God for

their interpreter! who not only understands what they do, but what they would say. Daniel could tell the meaning of the dream which Nebuchadnezzar had forgotten. God knows the meaning of those groans which never as yet knew their own meaning, and understands the sense of those sighs which never understood themselves.

Ejaculations, their use.—Ejaculations are short prayers darted up to God on emergent occasions. If no other artillery had been used this last seven years in England, I will not affirm more souls had been in heaven, but fewer corpses had been buried in earth. Oh that, with David, we might have said, 'My heart is fixed,' being less busied about fixing of muskets.

The principal use of ejaculations is against the fiery darts of the devil. Our adversary injects (*how* he doth it God knows, *that* he doth it we know) bad motions into our hearts, and that we may be as nimble with our antidotes as he with poisons, such short prayers are proper and necessary. In hard havens, so choked up with the envious sands that great ships drawing many foot water cannot come near, lighter and lesser pinnaces may freely and safely arrive. When we are time-bound, place-bound, or person-bound, so that we cannot compose ourselves to make a large solemn prayer, this is the right instant for ejaculations, whether orally uttered, or only poured forth inwardly in the heart.

Their privilege.—Ejaculations take not up any room in the soul. They give liberty of callings, so that at the same instant one may follow his proper vocation. The husbandman may dart forth an ejaculation, and not make a balk the more. The seaman, nevertheless, steers his ship right in the darkest night. Yea, the soldier at the same time may shoot out his prayer to God, and aim his pistol at his enemy, the one better hitting the mark for the other.

The field wherein bees feed is no whit the barer for their biting; when they have took their full repast on flower or grass, the ox may feed, the sheep fat on their reversions. The reason is, because those little chemists distil only the refined part of the flower, leaving the grosser substance thereof. So ejaculations bind not men to any bodily observance, only busy the spiritual half, which maketh them consistent with the prosecution of any other employment.

Extemporary prayers.—In extemporary prayer, what men most admire God least regardeth, namely, the volubility of the tongue. Herein a Tertullus may equal, yea, exceed St. Paul himself, 'whose speech was but mean.'' Oh, it is the heart keeping time and tune with the voice which God listeneth unto. Otherwise the nimblest tongue tires, and loudest voice grows dumb, before it comes halfway to heaven. Make it (said God to Moses) in all things like the pattern in the Mount (Heb. viii. 5). Only the conformity of the words with the mind, mounted in heavenly thoughts, is acceptable to God. The gift of extemporary prayer and ready utterance may be bestowed on a reprobate, but the grace thereof (religious affections) is only given to God's servants.

Their causeless scandal.—Some lay it to the charge of extemporary prayers, as if it were a diminution to God's majesty to offer them unto Him, because (alluding to David's expression to Ornan the Jebusite) they cost nothing, but come without any pains or industry to provide them (2 Sam. xxiv. 24). A most false aspersion.

Surely preparation of the heart (though not pre-meditation of every word), is required thereunto. And grant the party, praying at that very instant, forestudieth not only expression, yet surely he hath formerly laboured with his heart and tongue too, before he attained that dexterity of utterance, properly and readily to express himself. Many hours in night no doubt he is waking, and was, by himself, practising Scripture phrase and the language of Canaan, whilst such as censure him for his laziness were fast asleep in their beds.

Suppose one should make an entertainment for strangers with flesh, fish, fowl, venison, fruit, all out of his own fold, field, ponds, park, orchard, will any say that this feast cost him nothing who makes it? Surely, although all grew on the same, and for the present he bought nothing by the penny, yet he, or his ancestors for him, did at first dearly purchase home accommodations, from whence this entertainment did arise.

So the party who hath attained the faculty and facility of extemporary prayer (the easy act of a laborious habit), though at the instant not appearing to take pains, hath been formerly industrious with himself, or his parents with him, in giving him pious education, or else he had never acquired so great perfection, seeing only long practice makes the pen of a ready writer,

Night-prayer.—Death in Scripture is compared to sleep. Well, then, may my night-prayer be resembled to making my will. I will be careful not to die intestate, as also not to defer my will-making till I am not *compos mentis,* till the lethargy of drowsiness seize upon me.

But being in perfect memory, I bequeath my soul to God, the rather because I am sure the devil will accuse me when sleeping. Oh, the advantage of spirits above bodies! If our clay cottage be not cooled with rest, the roof falls afire. Satan hath no such need; the night is his fittest time. Thus man's vacation is the term for the beasts of the forest; they move most whilst he lies quiet in his bed.

Lest, therefore, whilst sleeping I be outlawed for want of appearance to Satan's charge, I commit my cause to him who neither slumbers nor sleeps. 'ANSWER FOR ME, O MY GOD.'

A nocturnal.—David, surveying the firmament, brake forth into this consideration: 'When I considered the heavens, the work of thy fingers, the moon and the stars, which thou hast created, what is man,' etc. (Psalm viii. 3).

How cometh he to mention the moon and stars, and omit the sun, the other being but his pensioners, shining with that exhibition of light, which the bounty of the sun allots them.

It is answered, this was David's night meditation, when the sun, departing to the other world, left the lesser light only visible in heaven, and as the sky is best beheld by day in the glory thereof, so it is best surveyed by night in the variety of the same.

Night was made for man to rest in. But when I cannot sleep, may I, with this psalmist, entertain my waking with good thoughts; not to use them as opium, to invite my corrupt nature to slumber, but to bolt out bad thoughts, which otherwise would possess my soul.

Set prayers.—Set prayers are prescript forms of our own or others' composing; such are lawful for any, and needful for some to use.

Lawful for any. Otherwise God would not have appointed the priests (presumed of themselves best able to pray) a form of blessing the people. Nor would our Saviour have set us his prayer, which (as the town-bushel is the standard both to measure corn and other bushels by) is both a prayer in itself and a pattern or platform of prayer. Such as accuse set forms to be pinioning the wings of the dove, will by the next return affirm that girdles and garters, made to strengthen and adorn, are so many shackles and fetters which hurt and hinder men's free motion.

Needful for some. Namely for such who as yet have not attained (what all should endeavour) to pray extempore by the spirit. But as little children (to whom the plainest and evenest room at first is a labyrinth) are so ambitious of going alone, that they scorn to take the guidance of a form or bench to direct them, but will adventure by themselves, though often to the cost of a knock and a fall; so many confess their weakness, in denying to confess it, who, refusing to be beholden to a set form of prayer, prefer to say nonsense, rather than nothing, in their extempore expressions. More modesty, and no less piety, it had been for such men to have prayed longer with set forms that they might pray better without them.

The same again.—It is no base and beggarly shift (arguing a narrow and necessitous heart), but a piece of holy and heavenly thrift, often to use the same prayer again. Christ's practice is my directory herein, who the third time said the same words.

A good prayer is not like a stratagem of war, to be used but once. No, the oftener the better. The clothes of the Israelites, whilst they wandered forty years in the wilderness, never waxed old, as if made of *perpetuano* indeed. So a good prayer, though often used, is still fresh and fair in the ears and eyes of heaven. Despair not then, thou simple soul, who hast no exchange of raiment, whose prayers cannot appear every day at heaven's court in new clothes. Thou mayest be as good a subject, though not so great a gallant, coming always in the same suit—yea, perchance the very same which was thy father's and grandfather's before thee (a well-composed prayer is a good heirloom in a family, and may hereditarily be descended to many generations), but know thy comfort, thy prayer is well known to heaven, to which it is a constant customer. Only add new, or new degrees of old affections thereunto, and it will be acceptable to God, thus repaired, as if new erected.

Prayer must be quotidian.—Among other arguments inforcing the necessity of daily prayer, this not the least, that Christ, enjoins us to petition for daily bread. New bread we know is best, and in a spiritual sense our bread, though in itself as stale and mouldy as that of the Gibeonites, is every day new, because a new and hot blessing, as I might say, is daily begged, and bestowed of God upon it.

Manna must daily be gathered, and not provisionally be hoarded up. God expects that men every day address themselves unto him by petitioning him for sustenance.

How contrary is this to the common practice of many. As camels in sandy countries are said to drink but once in seven days, and then for time past, present, and to come; so, many fumble this, last, and next week's devotion all in a prayer; yea, some defer all their praying till the last day.

Constantine had a conceit, that because baptism washed away all sins, he would not be baptized till his death-bed, that so his soul might never lose the purity thereof, but immediately mount to heaven. But sudden death preventing him, he was not baptized at all, as some say, or only by an Arian Bishop, as others affirm. If any erroneously, on the same supposition, put off their prayers to the last, let them take heed, lest long delayed, at last they prove either none at all, or none in effect.

The Lord's prayer.—In this age we begin to think meanly of the Lord's prayer. Oh, how basely may the Lord think of our prayers! Some will not forgive the Lord's prayer for that passage therein, ' As we forgive them that trespass against us.'

Others play the witches on this prayer. Witches are reported (amongst many other hellish observations, whereby they oblige themselves to Satan) to say the Lord's prayer backwards. Are there not many, who though they do not pronounce the syllables of the

Lord's prayer retrograde (their discretion will not
suffer them to be betrayed to such a nonsense sin),
yet they transpose it in effect, desiring their daily
bread before God's kingdom come, preferring temporal
benefits before heavenly blessings. Oh! if every one
by this mark should be tried for a witch, how hard
would it go with all of us.

All best.—At the siege and taking of New Carthage, in Spain, there was dissension betwixt the
soldiers about the crown-mural due to him who first
footed the walls of the city. Two pretended to the
crown ; parts were taken, and the Roman army, siding
in factions, was likely to fall foul, and mutually fight
against itself. Scipio, the general, prevented the
danger by providing two mural crowns, giving one to
each who claimed it, affirming, that on the examina-
tion of the proofs, both did appear to him at the same
instant to climb the wall. Oh, let us not set several
kinds of prayers at variance betwixt themselves, which
of them should be most useful, most honourable. All
are most excellent at several times, crown-groans,
crown-ejaculations, crown-extemporary, crown-set,
crown-mixed prayer, I dare boldly say, he that in
some measure loves not all kind of lawful prayers,
loves no kind of lawful prayers. For if we love God
the father, we can hate no ordinance, his child, though
perchance an occasion may affect one above another.

All manner of prayers.—It is an ancient stratagem of Satan (yet still he useth it, still men are
cheated by it) to set God's ordinance at variance, as
the disciples fell out amongst themselves which of
them should be the greatest. How hath the reader's

pew been clashed against the preacher's pulpit, to the shaking almost of the whole church, whether that the word preached or read be most effectual to salvation. Also, whether the word preached or catechised most useful. But no ordinance so abused as prayer. Prayer hath been set up against preaching, against cate-chising, against itself. Whether public or private, church or closet, set or extemporary prayer be the best. See how St. Paul determines the controversy, πάσῃ προσευχῇ, 'with all manner of prayer and supplication in the Spirit' (so the Geneva translation): preferring none, commending all lawful prayer to our practice.

To God alone.—Amongst all manner of prayer to God, I find in Scripture neither promise, precept, nor precedent to warrant prayers to saints. And were there no other reason, this would encourage me to pray to Christ alone—because St. Paul struck Elimas blind, Christ made blind Bartimæus see. St. Peter killed Ananias and Sapphira with his word, Christ with his word revived dead Lazarus. The disciples forbade the Syrophœnician woman to call after Christ, Christ called unto her after they had forbidden her. All my Saviour's works are saving works, none ex-tending to the death of mankind. Surely Christ, being now in heaven, hath not less goodness because he hath more glory; his bowels still yearn on us. I will therefore rather present my prayers to him, who always did heal, than to those who sometimes did hurt. And though this be no convincing argument to Papists, it is a comfortable motive to Protestants. A good third, where so good firsts and seconds have been laid before.

OCCASIONAL MEDITATIONS.

Love and anger.—I saw two children fighting together in the street. The father of the one, passing by, fetched his son away, and corrected him; the other lad was left without any check, though both were equally faulty in the fray. I was half offended, that being guilty alike, they were not punished alike; but the parent would only meddle with him over whom he had an undoubted dominion, to whom he bare an unfeigned affection.

The wicked sin, the godly smart, most in this world. God singleth out his own sons, and beateth them by themselves: whom 'he loveth he chasteneth,' whilst the ungodly, preserved from affliction, are, reserved for destruction, it being needless that their hair should be shaved with a hired razor (Isaiah vii. 20) whose heads are intended for the axe of divine justice (Matt. iii. 10).

Upwards, upwards.—How large houses do they build in London on little ground; revenging themselves on the narrowness of their room with store of stories! Excellent arithmetic! from the root of one floor, to multiply so many chambers. And though painful the climbing up, pleasant the staying there, the higher the healthier, with clear light and sweeter air.

Small are my means on earth. May I mount my soul the higher in heavenly meditations, relying on Divine providence. He that fed many thousands with five loaves, may feed me and mine with the fifth part of that one loaf. Higher, my soul! higher! In bodily buildings, commonly the garrets are most empty; but my mind, the higher mounted, will be the better furnished. Let perseverance to death be my uppermost chamber, the roof of which grace is the pavement of glory.

Beware wanton wit.—I saw an indenture too fairly engrossed, for the writer (better scrivener than clerk) had so filled it with flourishes that it hindered my reading thereof; the wantonness of his pen made a new alphabet, and I was subject to mistake his dashes for real letters.

What damage hath unwary rhetoric done to religion ! Many an innocent reader hath taken Damascene and Theophilact at their word, counting their eloquent hyperboles of Christ's presence in the sacrament the exact standards of their judgment, whence after-ages brought in transubstantiation. Yea, from the fathers' elegant apostrophes to the dead (lively pictures by hasty eyes may be taken for living persons) prayers to saints took their original. I see that truth's secretary must use a set hand in writing important points of divinity. Ill dancing for nimble wits, on the precipices of dangerous doctrines, for though they escape by their agility, others (encouraged by their examples) may be brought to destruction.

Ill done, undone.—I saw one, whether out of haste or want of skill, put up his sword the wrong way; it cut, even when it was sheathed, the edge being transposed where the back should have been, so that, perceiving his error, he was fain to draw it out, that he might put it up again.

Wearied and wasted with civil war, we that formerly

loathed the manna of peace, because common, could now be content to feed on it, though full of worms and putrified. Some so desirous thereof, that they care not on what terms the war be ended, so it be ended; but such a peace would be but a truce, and the conditions thereof would no longer be in force, than whilst they are in force. Let us pray that the sword be sheathed the right way, with God's glory and without the dangerous dislocation of prince and people's right, otherwise it may justly be suspected that the sword put up will be drawn out again, and the articles of an ill agreement, though engrossed on parchment, not take effect so long as paper would continue.

Apace, apace.—Rowing on the Thames, the waterman confirmed me in what formerly I had learnt from the maps, how that river, westward, runs so crooked as likely to lose itself in a labyrinth of its own making. From Reading to London, by land thirty, by water an hundred miles. So wantonly that stream disporteth itself, as if as yet unresolved whether to advance to the sea or retreat to its fountain.

But the same being past London, as if sensible of its former laziness, and fearing to be checked of the ocean, the mother of all rivers, for so long loitering; or else, as if weary with wandering, and loth to lose more way; or lastly, as if conceiving such wildness inconsistent with the gravity of his channel, now grown old and ready to be buried in the sea, runs in so direct a line that from London to Gravesend the number of the miles are equally twenty, both by land and by water.

Alas! how much of my life is lavished away! Oh, the intricacies, windings, wanderings, turnings, tergiversations of my deceitful youth! I have lived in the midst of a crooked generation, and with them 'have turned aside unto crooked ways.' High time it is now for me to make straight paths for my feet, and to redeem what is past by amending what is present and to come. *Flux, flux* (in the German tongue, quick, quick) was a motto of Bishop Jewel's, presaging the approach of his death. May I make good use thereof; *make haste, make haste*, God knows how little time is left me, and may I be a good husband, to improve the short remnant thereof.

Always the rising sun.—I have wondered why the Romish church do not pray to St. Abraham, St. David, St. Hezekiah, etc., as well as to the apostles and their successors since Christ's time; for those ancient patriarchs, by the confession of Papists, were long since relieved out of limbo (soon out, who were never in), and admitted to the sight and presence of God, especially Abraham, being father of the faithful, as well Gentile as Jew, would (according to their principles) be a proper patron for their petitions.

But it seems that modern saints rob the old ones of their honour; a Garnet, or Bernard of Paris, have severally more prayers made unto them than many old saints have together. New besoms sweep clean; new cisterns of fond men's own hewing, most likely to hold water.

Protestants in some kind serve their living ministers, as Papists their dead saints. For aged pastors, who have borne the heat of the day in our church, are jostled out of respect by young preachers, not having half their age, nor a quarter of learning and religion. Yet let not the former be disheartened, for thus it ever was and will be: English Athenians, all for novelties, new sects, new schisms, new doctrines, new disciplines, new prayers, new preachers.

Charity, charity.—Church story reports of St. John that, being grown very aged (well nigh a hundred years old), wanting strength and voice to make a long sermon, he was wont to go up into the pulpit, and often repeat these words: 'Babes, keep yourselves from idols; brethren, love one another.'

Our age may seem sufficiently to have provided against the growth of idolatry in England. Oh, that some order were taken for the increase of charity. It were liberty enough, if for the next seven years all sermons were bound to keep residence on this text, ' Brethren, love one another.'

But would not some fall out with themselves, if appointed to preach unity to others? Vindictive spirits, if confined to this text, would confine the text to their passion; by brethren, understanding only such of their own party. But O! seeing other monopolies are dissolved, let not this remain against the fundamental law of charity. Let all bend their heads, hearts, and hands, to make up the breaches in Church and State. But too many nowadays are like Pharaoh's magicians who could conjure up with their charms more new frogs, but could not remove or drive away those multitudes of frogs which were there before. Unhappily happy in making more rents and dissensions, but unable or unwilling to compose our former differences.

Christ my King.—I read how King Edward I. ingeniously surprised the Welsh into subjection, proffering them such a prince as should be,

1. The son of a king;
2. Born in their own country;
3. Whom none could tax for any fault.

The Welsh accepted the conditions, and the king tendered them his son Edward, an infant, newly born in the Castle of Carnarvon.

Do not all these qualifications mystically centre themselves in my Saviour?

1. The King of heaven saith unto him, 'Thou art my Son, this day have I begotten thee;'
2. Our true countryman, real flesh, whereas he took not on him the nature of angels;
3. Without spot or blemish, like to us in all things, sin only excepted.

Away then with those wicked men who will not have this King to rule over them. May he have dominion in, and over me. 'Thy kingdom come.' Heaven and earth cannot afford a more proper prince for the purpose, exactly accomplished with all these comfortable qualifications.

Tribulations.—I find two sad etymologies of tribulation. One from *tribulus*, a three-forked thorn, which intimates that such afflictions which are as full of pain and anguish to the soul as a thorn thrust into a tender part of the flesh is unto the body, may properly be termed tribulations.

The other, from *tribulus*, the head of a flail, or flagel, knaggy and knotty (made commonly, as I take it, of a thick blackthorn), and then it imports that afflictions, falling upon us as heavy as the flail threshing the corn, are styled tribulations.

I am in a strait which deduction to embrace, from the sharp or from the heavy thorn. But which is the worst, though I may choose whence to derive the word, I cannot choose so as to decline the thing, 'I must through much tribulation enter into the kingdom of God.'

Therefore I will labour not to be like a young colt first set to plough, which more tires himself out with his own untowardness, whipping himself with his misspent mettle, than with the weight of what he draws; and will labour patiently to bear what is imposed upon me.

Beware.—I saw a cannon shot off. The men at whom it was levelled fell flat on the ground, and so escaped the bullet. Against such blows, falling is all the fencing, and prostration all the armour of proof.

But that which gave them notice to fall down, was their perceiving of the fire before the ordnance was discharged. Oh the mercy of that fire ! which, as it were, repenting of the mischief it had done, and the murder it might make, ran a race and outstripped the bullet, that men (at the sight thereof) might be provided, when they could not resist to prevent it. Thus every murdering-piece is also a warning-piece against itself.

God, in like manner, warns before he wounds; frights before he fights. 'Yet forty days and Nineveh shall be overthrown' (Jonah iii. 4). Oh let us fall down before the Lord our Maker. Then shall His anger be pleased to make in us a daily pass-over, and His bullets levelled at us must fly above us.

The recruit.—I read how one main argument which the Apostle Paul enforceth on Timothy, to make full proof of his ministry, is this, 'For I am now ready to be offered, and the time of my departure is at hand' (2 Tim. iv. 6). Thus the dying saints, drawing near to heaven, their mark is the best spur for the surviving to make the more speed in their race.

How many excellent divines have these sad times hastened to their long home (so called in Scripture, not because long going thither, but long tarrying there)! How many have been sorrow-shot to their heart! Oh that this would edge the endeavours of our generation to succeed in the dead places of worthy men. Shall the Papists curiously observe and sufficiently boast that their Stapleton was born on the same day on which Sir Thomas More was beheaded (as if his cradle made the other's coffin), and shall not our nurseries of learning supply the void room of our worthies deceased? No sin, I hope, to pray that our Timothys come not short of our Pauls; as in time, so in learning and religion.

Edification.—I read in a learned physician how our provident mother, Nature, foreseeing men (her wanton children) would be tampering with the edge-tools of minerals, hid them far from them, in the bowels of the earth; whereas she exposed plants and herbs more obvious to their eye as fitter for their use. But some bold empirics, neglecting the latter (as too common), have adventured on those hidden minerals, ofttimes (through want of skill) to the hurt of many, and hazard of more.

God, in the New Testament, hath placed all historical and practical matter (needful for Christians to know and believe) in the beginning of the Gospel. All such truths lay above ground, plainly visible in the literal sense. The prophetical and difficult part comes in the close; but though the Testament was written in Greek, too many read it like Hebrew, beginning at the end thereof. How many trouble themselves about the Revelation who might be better busied in plain divinity! Safer prescribing to others, and practising in themselves, positive piety; leaving such mystical minerals to men of more judgment to prepare them.

Mad, not mad.—I find St. Paul in the same chapter confess and deny madness in himself (Acts xxvi. 11): 'And being exceeding mad against them, I persecuted them even unto strange cities.' When Festus challenged him to be beside himself, 'I am not mad, most noble Festus' (ver. 25). Whilst he was mad indeed, then none did suspect or accuse him to be distracted; but when converted, and in his right mind, then Festus taxeth him of madness.

There is a country in Africa wherein all the natives have pendulous lips, hanging down like a dog's ears, always raw and sore. Here only such as are handsome are pointed at for monsters in this age, wherein polluted and unclean lips are grown epidemical. If any refrain their tongues from common sins, they alone are gazed at as strange spectacles.

The deepest cut.—I beheld a lapidary cutting a diamond with a diamond hammer and anvil both of the same kind.

God in Scripture styled his servants his jewels. His

diamonds they are, but, alas! rude, rough, unpolished, without shape or fashion, as they arise naked out of the bed of the earth, before art hath dressed them. See how God, by rubbing one rough diamond against another, maketh both smooth. Barnabas afflicts Paul, and Paul afflicts Barnabas, by their hot falling out (Acts xv. 39); Jerome occasioneth trouble to Rufinus, and Rufinus to Jerome.

In our unnatural war none I hope so weak and wilful as to deny many good men (though misled) engaged on both sides. Oh! how have they scratched, and raced, and pierced, and bruised, and broken one another! Behold heaven's hand grating one diamond with another. As for all those who uncharitably deny any good on that party which they dislike, such show themselves diamonds indeed in their hardness (cruel censuring), but none in any commendable quality in their conditions.

THE HOLY STATE AND THE PROFANE STATE.

'In that day shall there be upon the bells of the horses, HOLINESS UNTO THE LORD.'—ZECHARIAH xiv. 20.

'The vile person shall be no more called liberal, nor the churl said to be bountiful.'—ISAIAH xxxii. 5.

'And they shall teach my people the difference betwixt the holy and profane.'—EZEKIEL xliv. 23.

The Holy and the Profane State seems to have been written by Fuller whilst Rector of Broad-Windsor, and to have been sent to press in the year 1640. It was not published, however, till 1642, by which time he had removed to London, and was preacher at the Savoy. During this interval many changes had happened both in Church and State, and the political convulsions of the time were rapidly approaching their crisis. To this he alludes in his preface to the reader : ' Be pleased to know, that when I left my home it was fair weather, and my journey was half passed before I discovered the tempest, and had gone so far in this book that I could neither go backward with credit nor forward with comfort.' He requests his readers to exercise discretion and charity in their judgment of his work : ' And I conjure thee, by all Christian ingenuity, that if lighting here on some passage rather harsh sounding than ill intended, to construe the same by the general drift and main scope which is aimed at.'

It consists of five books, of which the first four delineate the Holy, the fifth and last, the Profane State. These are divided into a hundred and five sections, in each of which some type of character is described either by aphoristic sentences, by an illustrative narrative, or by both. The selections which follow will suffice to show the general mode of treatment.

It gained a speedy and immense popularity. He complains, however, that ' as some unmarried maids will never be more than eighteen,' so ' for some design of the stationer' this, as well as some other of his works, ' sticketh still, in the title page, at the third edition, yet hath it oftener passed the press.' The design of the publisher in thus understating the numbers sold, is uncertain. It probably arose from a fear of attracting the attention of the authorities to the book, as it contains many passages which might be understood in a sense unfavourable to the revolutionary government.

He showeth his children, in his own practice, what to follow and imitate; and, in others, what to shun and avoid. For though 'the words of the wise be as nails fastened by the masters of the assemblies' (Eccles. xii. 11), yet, sure, their examples are the hammer to drive them in, to take the deeper hold. A father that whipped his son for swearing, and swore himself whilst he whipped him, did more harm by his example than good by his correction.

He doth not welcome and embrace the first essays of sin in his children. Weeds are counted herbs in the beginning of the spring: nettles are put in pottage, and salads are made of eldern-buds. Thus fond fathers like the oaths and wanton talk of their little children; and please themselves to hear them displease God. But our wise parent both instructs his children in piety, and with correction blasts the first buds of profaneness in them. He that will not use the rod on his child, his child shall be used as a rod on him.

He allows his children maintenance according to their quality. Otherwise it will make them base, acquaint them with bad company and sharking tricks; and it makes them surfeit the sooner when they come to their estates. It is observed of camels, that, having travelled long without water through sandy deserts, *implentur, cùm bibendi est occasio, et in prœteritum et in futurum:* [1] and so these thirsty heirs soak it when they come to their means, who, whilst their fathers were living, might not touch the top of their money, and think they shall never feel the bottom of it when they are dead.

In choosing a profession he is directed by his child's disposition, whose inclination is the strongest indenture to bind him to a trade. But when they set Abel to till the ground, and send Cain to keep sheep; Jacob to hunt, and Esau to live in tents; drive some to school, and others from it; they commit a violence on nature, and it will thrive accordingly. Yet he humours not his child when he makes an unworthy choice beneath himself, or rather for ease than use, pleasure than profit.

If his son prove wild, he doth not cast him off so far, but he marks the place where he lights. With the mother of Moses, he doth not suffer his son so to sink or swim, but he leaves one to stand afar off to watch what will become of him (Exod. ii. 4). He is careful, whilst he quencheth his luxury, not withal to put out his life; the rather, because their souls who have broken and run out in their youth, have proved the more healthful for it afterwards.

He moves him to marriage rather by argument drawn from his good, than his own authority. It is a style too princely for a parent herein to 'will and command;' but, sure, he may will and desire. Affections, like the conscience, are rather to be led than drawn;

---

[1] 'When they find an opportunity they fill themselves both for the past and the future.'

and, it is to be feared, they that marry where they do not love, will love where they do not marry.

He doth not give away his loaf to his children, and then come to them for a piece of bread. He holds the reins (though loosely) in his own hands; and keeps, to reward duty, and punish undutifulness. Yet, on good occasion, for his children's advancement, he will depart from part of his means. Base is their nature who will not have their branches lopped, till their body be felled; and will let go none of their goods, as if it presaged their speedy death: whereas it doth not follow that he that puts off his cloak must presently go to bed.

On his death-bed he bequeaths his blessing to all his children. Nor rejoiceth he so much to leave them great portions, as honestly obtained. Only money well and lawfully gotten is good and lawful money. And if he leaves his children young, he principally nominates God to be their guardian; and, next Him, is careful to appoint provident overseers.

THE GOOD CHILD.

HE reverenceth the person of his parent, though old, poor, and froward. As his parent bare with him when a child, he bears with his parent if twice a child; nor doth his dignity above him cancel his duty unto him. When Sir Thomas More was Lord Chancellor of England, and Sir John his father one of the Judges of the King's Bench, he would in Westminster-hall beg his blessing of him on his knees.

He observes his lawful commands, and practiseth his

precepts, with all obedience. I cannot, therefore, excuse St. Barbara from undutifulness, and occasioning her own death. The matter this: Her father, being a Pagan, commanded his workmen, building his house, to make two windows in a room. Barbara, knowing her father's pleasure, in his absence enjoined them to make three, that, seeing them, she might the better contemplate the mystery of the Holy Trinity. Methinks, two windows might as well have raised her meditations, and the light arising from both would as properly have minded her of the Holy Spirit proceeding from the Father and the Son. Her father, enraged, at his return, thus came to the knowledge of her religion, and accused her to the magistrate; which cost her her life.

Having practised them himself, he entails his parents' precepts on his posterity. Therefore such instructions are by Solomon (Prov. i. 9) compared to frontlets and chains (not to a suit of clothes, which serves but one, and quickly wears out, or out of fashion), which have in them a real lasting worth, and are bequeathed as legacies to another age. The same counsels, observed, are chains to grace; which, neglected, prove halters to strangle undutiful children.

He is a stork to his parent, and feeds him in his old age. Not only if his father hath been a pelican, but though he hath been an ostrich unto him, and neglected him in his youth. He confines him not a long way off to a short pension, forfeited if he comes in his presence; but shows piety at home, and learns (as St. Paul saith, 1 Tim. v. 4) to requite his parent. And yet the debt (I mean only the principal, not counting the interest) cannot fully be paid; and therefore he compounds with his father to accept in good worth the utmost of his endeavour.

Such a child God commonly rewards with long life in this world. If he chance to die young, yet he lives long that lives well; and time mis-spent is not lived but lost. Besides, God is better than his promise, if he takes him a long lease, and gives him a freehold of better value. As for disobedient children,—

If preserved from the gallows, they are reserved for the rack, to be tortured by their own posterity. One complained that never father had so undutiful a child as he had. 'Yes,' said his son, with less grace than truth, 'my grandfather had.'

I conclude this subject with the example of a Pagan's son, which will shame most Christians. Pomponius Atticus, making the funeral oration at the death of his mother, did protest, that, living with her threescore and seven years, he was never reconciled unto her, *se nunquam cum matre in gratiam redisse ;* because (take the comment with the text) there never happened betwixt them the least jar which needed reconciliation.

THE GOOD MASTER.

HE is the heart in the midst of his household, first up and last a-bed, if not in his person, yet in his providence. In his carriage he aimeth at his own and his servants' good, and to advance both.

He oversees the works of his servants. One said,

that 'the dust that fell from the master's shoes was the best compost to manure ground.' The lion, out of state, will not run whilst any one looks upon him; but some servants, out of slothfulness, will not run except some do look upon them, spurred on with their master's eye. Chiefly he is careful exactly to take his servants' reckonings. If their master takes no account of them, they will make small account of him, and care not what they spend who are never brought to an audit.

He provides them victuals, wholesome, sufficient, and seasonable. He doth not so alloy his servants' bread, or debase it so much, as to make that servants' meat which is not man's meat. He alloweth them also convenient rest and recreation: whereas some masters, like a bad conscience, will not suffer them to sleep that have them. He remembers the old law of the Saxon king Ina: 'If a villain work on Sunday by his lord's command, he shall be free.'

The wages he contracts for, he duly and truly pays to his servants. The same word in the Greek, *iós*, signifies 'rust' and 'poison:' and some strong poison is made of the rust of metals; but none more venomous than the rust of money in the rich man's purse unjustly detained from the labourer, which will poison and infect his whole estate.

He never threatens (Ephes. vi. 9) his servant, but rather presently corrects him. Indeed, conditional threatenings, with promise of pardon on amendment, are good and useful. Absolute threatenings torment more, reform less, making servants keep their faults and forsake their masters: wherefore, herein he never passeth his word, but makes present payment, lest the creditor run away from the debtor.

In correcting his servant, he becomes not a slave to his own passion. Not cruelly making new indentures of the flesh of his apprentice. To this end, he never beats him in the height of his passion. Moses, being to fetch water out of the rock, and commanded by God only to speak to it with his rod in his hand, being transported with anger, smote it thrice. Thus some masters, who might fetch penitent tears from their servants with a chiding word (only shaking the rod withal for terror), in their fury strike many blows which might better be spared. If he perceives his servant incorrigible, so that he cannot wash the blackamoor, he washeth his hands of him, and fairly puts him away.

He is tender of his servant in sickness and age. If crippled in his service, his house is his hospital. Yet how many throw away those dry bones out of which themselves have sucked the marrow! It is as usual to see a young serving-man an old beggar, as to see a light-horse, first from the great saddle of a nobleman, to come to the hackney-coach, and at last die in drawing a cart. But the good master is not like the cruel hunter in the fable, who beat his old dog because his toothless mouth let go the game. He rather imitates the noble nature of our prince Henry, who took order for the keeping of an old English mastiff which had made a lion run away. Good reason good service in age should be rewarded. Who can without pity and pleasure behold that trusty vessel which carried Sir Francis Drake about the world?

THE GOOD SERVANT.

He is one that, out of conscience, serves God in his master; and so hath the principle of obedience in himself. As for those servants who found their obedience on some external thing, with engines, they will go no longer than they are wound or weighed up.

He doth not dispute his master's lawful will, but doth it. Hence it is that simple servants (understand such whose capacity is bare measure, without surplusage, equal to the business they are used in) are more useful, because more manageable, than abler men, especially in matters wherein not their brains but hands are required. Yet if his master, out of want of experience, enjoins him to do what is hurtful and prejudicial to his own estate, duty here makes him undutiful (if not to deny, to demur in his performance), and, choosing rather to displease than hurt his master, he humbly represents his reasons to the contrary.

He loves to go about his business with cheerfulness. One said he loved to hear his carter, though not his cart, to sing. 'God loveth a cheerful giver:' and Christ reproved the Pharisees for disfiguring their faces with a sad countenance. Fools, who, to persuade men that angels lodged in their hearts, hung out a devil for a sign in their faces! Sure, cheerfulness in doing renders a deed more acceptable. Not like those servants, who doing their work unwillingly, their looks do enter a protestation against what their hands are doing.

He despatcheth his business with quickness and

expedition. Hence the same English word 'speed' signifies 'celerity' and 'success;' the former, in business of execution, causing the latter. Indeed, haste and rashness are storms and tempests, breaking and wrecking business : but nimbleness is a fair, full wind, blowing it with speed to the haven. As he is good at hand, so he is good at length, continually and constantly careful in his service. Many servants, as if they had learned the nature of the besoms they use, are good for a few days, and afterwards grow unserviceable.

He disposeth not of his master's goods without his privity or consent. No, not in the smallest matters. Open this wicket, and it will be in vain for masters to shut the door. If servants presume to dispose small things without their masters' allowance, (besides that many little leaks may sink a ship!) this will widen their consciences to give away greater. But though he hath not always a particular leave, he hath a general grant, and a warrant dormant, from his master to give an alms to the poor in his absence, if in absolute necessity.

His answers to his master are true, direct, and dutiful. If a dumb devil possesseth a servant, a winding cane is the fittest circle, and the master the exorcist to drive it out. Some servants are so talkative, one may as well command the echo as them not to speak last ; and then they count themselves conquerors, because they last leave the field. Others, though they seem to yield, and go away, yet, with the flying Parthians, shoot backward over their shoulders, and dart bitter taunts at their masters ; yea, though, with the clock, they have given the last stroke, yet they keep a jarring, muttering to themselves a good while after.

Because charity is so cold, his industry is the hotter to provide something for himself, whereby he may be maintained in his old age. If, under his master, he trades for himself (as an apprentice may do, if he hath covenanted so beforehand), he provides good bounds and sufficient fences betwixt his own and his master's estate (Jacob ' set his flock three days' journey' from Laban's, Gen. xxx. 36), that no quarrel may arise about their property, nor suspicion that his remnant hath eaten up his master's whole cloth.

THE FAITHFUL MINISTER.

HE endeavours to get the general love and good-will of his parish. This he doth, not so much to make a benefit *of* them, as a benefit *for* them, that his ministry may be more effectual; otherwise he may preach his own heart out, before he preacheth anything into theirs. The good conceit of the physician is half a cure; and his practice will scarce be happy where his person is hated. Yet he humours them not in his doctrine, to get their love; for such a spaniel is worse than a dumb dog. He shall sooner get their good-will by walking uprightly than by crouching and creeping. If pious living and painful labouring in his calling will not win their affections, he counts it gain to lose them. As for those who causelessly hate him, he pities and prays for them : and such there will be. I should suspect his preaching had no salt in it, if no galled horse did wince.

He is strict in ordering his conversation. As for those who cleanse blurs with blotted fingers, they make it the worse. It was said of one who preached very well, and lived very ill, 'that when he was out of the pulpit, it was pity he should ever go into it; and when he was in the pulpit, it was pity he should ever come out of it.' But our minister *lives* sermons. And yet I deny not, but dissolute men, like unskilful horsemen, who open a gate on the wrong side, may, by the virtue of their office, open heaven for others, and shut themselves out.

His behaviour towards his people is grave and courteous. Not too austere and retired; which is laid to the charge of good Mr. Hooper the martyr, that his rigidness frighted people from consulting with him. 'Let your light,' saith Christ, 'shine before men;' whereas over-reservedness makes the brightest virtue burn dim. Especially he detesteth affected gravity (which is rather *on* men than *in* them), whereby some belie their register-book, antedate their age to seem far older than they are, and plait and set their brows in an affected sadness. Whereas St. Anthony the monk might have been known among hundreds of his order by his cheerful face, he having ever, though a most mortified man, a merry countenance.

He doth not clash God's ordinances together about precedency. Not making odious comparisons betwixt prayer and preaching, preaching and catechising, public prayer and private, premeditate prayer and *ex tempore*. When, at the taking of New Carthage in Spain, two soldiers contended about the mural crown, due to him who first climbed the walls, so that the whole army was thereupon in danger of division; Scipio the general said, he knew that they both got up the wall together, and so gave the scaling crown to them both. Thus our minister compounds all controversies betwixt God's ordinances, by praising them all, practising them all, and thanking God for them all. He counts the reading of Common Prayers to prepare him the better for preaching; and, as one said, if he did first toll the bell on one side, it made it afterwards ring out the better in his sermons.

He carefully catechiseth his people in the elements of religion. Except he hath (a rare thing!) a flock without lambs, of all old sheep; and yet even Luther did not scorn to profess himself *discipulum Catechismi,* 'a scholar of the Catechism.' By this catechising, the Gospel first got ground of Popery: and let not our religion, now grown rich, be ashamed of that which first gave it credit and set it up, lest the Jesuits beat us at our own weapon. Through the want of this catechising, many who are well skilled in some dark out-corners of divinity, have lost themselves in the beaten road thereof.

He will not offer to God of that which costs him nothing. But takes pains aforehand for his sermons. Demosthenes never made any oration on the sudden; yea, being called upon, he never rose up to speak, except he had well studied the matter: and he was wont to say, 'that he showed how he honoured and reverenced the people of Athens, because he was careful what he spake unto them.' Indeed, if our minister be surprised with a sudden occasion, he counts himself rather to be excused than commended, if, premeditating only the bones of his sermon, he clothes it with flesh *ex tempore.* As for those whose long custom hath made preaching their nature, [so] that they can discourse sermons without study, he accounts their examples rather to be admired than imitated.

Having brought his sermon into his head, he labours to bring it into his heart before he preaches it to his people. Surely, that preaching which comes from the soul most works on the soul. Some have questioned *ventriloquy,* when men strangely speak out of their bellies, whether it can be done lawfully or no: might I coin the word *cordiloquy,* when men draw the doctrines out of their hearts, sure, all would count this lawful and commendable.

He chiefly reproves the reigning sins of the time and place he lives in. We may observe, that our Saviour never inveighed against idolatry, usury, sabbath-breaking, amongst the Jews. Not that these were not sins, but they were not practised so much in that age, wherein wickedness was spun with a finer thread; and therefore Christ principally bent the drift of His preaching against spiritual pride, hypocrisy, and traditions, then predominant amongst the people, Also our minister confuteth no old heresies which time hath confuted; nor troubles his auditory with such strange hideous cases of conscience, that it is more hard to find the case than the resolution. In public reproving of sin, he ever whips the vice and spares the person.

He doth not only move the bread of life, and toss it up and down in generalities, but also breaks it into

particular directions. Drawing it down to cases of
conscience, that a man may be warranted in his particular actions, whether they be lawful or not. And he
teacheth people their lawful liberty, as well as their
restraints and prohibitions; for, amongst men, it is as
ill taken to turn back favours, as to disobey commands.

The places of Scripture he quotes are pregnant and
pertinent. As for heaping up of many quotations, it
smacks of a vain ostentation of memory. Besides, it
is as impossible that the hearer should profitably retain
them all, as that the preacher hath seriously perused
them all; yea, whilst the auditors stop their attention,
and stoop down to gather an impertinent quotation,
the sermon runs on, and they lose more substantial
matter.

His similes and illustrations are always familiar,
never contemptible. Indeed, reasons are the pillars
of the fabric of a sermon; but similitudes are the
windows which give the best lights. He avoids such
stories whose mention may suggest bad thoughts to
the auditors, and will not use a light comparison to
make thereof a grave application, for fear lest his
poison go farther than his antidote.

He provideth not only wholesome but plentiful food
for his people. Almost incredible was the painfulness
of Baronius, the compiler of the voluminous ' Annals
of the Church,' who, for thirty years together, preached
three or four times a-week to the people. As for our
minister, he preferreth rather to entertain his people
with wholesome cold meat which was on the table
before, than with that which is hot from the spit, raw

and half-roasted. Yet, in repetition of the same sermon, every edition hath a new addition, if not of new matter, of new affections. ' Of whom,' saith St. Paul, 'I have told you *often*, and *now* tell you even weeping' (Phil. iii. 18).

He makes not that wearisome, which should ever be welcome. Wherefore his sermons are of an ordinary length, except on an extraordinary occasion. What a gift had John Halsebach, Professor at Vienna, in tediousness! who, being to expound the Prophet Isaiah to his auditors, read twenty-one years on the first chapter, and yet finished it not.

He counts the success of his ministry the greatest preferment. Yet herein God hath humbled many painful pastors, in making them to be clouds to rain, not over Arabia the Happy, but over the Stony or Desert. Yet such pastors may comfort themselves, that great is their reward with God in heaven, who measures it, not by their success, but endeavours. Besides, though they see not, their people may feel, benefit by their ministry. Yea, the preaching of the word in some places is like the planting of woods, where, though no profit is received for twenty years together, it comes afterwards. And grant, that God honours thee not to build his temple in thy parish, yet thou mayest, with David, provide metal and materials for Solomon thy successor to build it with.

To sick folks he comes sometimes before he is sent for, as counting his vocation a sufficient calling. None of his flock shall want the extreme unction of prayer and counsel. Against the communion, especially, he endeavours that Janus's temple be shut in the whole parish, and that all be made friends.

He is never plaintiff in any suit but to be right's defendant. If his dues be detained from him, he grieves more for his parishioner's bad conscience than his own damage. He had rather suffer ten times in his profit, than once in his title, where not only his person, but posterity, is wronged; and then he proceeds fairly and speedily to a trial, that he may not vex and weary others, but right himself. During his suit he neither breaks off nor slacks offices of courtesy to his adversary; yea, though he loseth his suit, he will not also lose his charity.

He is moderate in his tenets and opinions. Not that he gilds over lukewarmness in matters of moment with the title of 'discretion;' but, withal, he is careful not to entitle violence, in indifferent and inconcerning matters, to be zeal. Indeed, men of extraordinary tallness, though otherwise little deserving, are made porters to lords; and those of unusual littleness are made ladies' dwarfs; whilst men of moderate stature may want masters. Thus many, notorious for extremities, may find favourers to prefer them; whilst moderate men in the middle truth may want any to advance them. But what saith the apostle? 'If in this life only we have hope in Christ, we are of all men most miserable' (1 Cor. xv. 19).

He is sociable and willing to do any courtesy for his neighbour-ministers. He willingly communicates his knowledge unto them. Surely, the gifts and graces of Christians lay in common, till base envy made the first enclosure. He neither slighteth his inferiors, nor repineth at those who in parts and credit are above him. He loveth the company of his neighbour-ministers. Sure, as ambergris is nothing so sweet in itself, as when it is compounded with other things, so both godly and learned men are gainers by communicating themselves to their neighbours.

Lying on his death-bed, he bequeaths to each of his parishioners his precepts and example for a legacy. And they, in requital, erect every one a monument for him in their hearts. He is so far from that base jealousy that his memory should be outshined by a brighter successor, and from that wicked desire that his people may find his worth by the worthlessness of him that succeeds, that he doth heartily pray to God to provide them a better pastor after his decease. As for outward estate, he commonly lives in too bare pasture to die fat. It is well if he hath gathered any flesh, being more in blessing than bulk.

OF SELF-PRAISING.

He whose own worth doth speak, need not speak his own worth. Such boasting sounds proceed from emptiness of desert: whereas the conquerors in the Olympian games did not put on the laurels on their own heads, but waited till some other did it. Only anchorets, that want company, may crown themselves with their own commendations.

It showeth more wit, but no less vanity, to commend one's self, not in a straight line, but by reflexion. Some sail to the port of their own praise by a side-

wind: as when they dispraise themselves, stripping
themselves naked of what is their due, that the
modesty of the beholders may clothe them with it
again; or when they flatter another to his face,
tossing the ball to him, that he may throw it back
again to them; or when they commend that
quality, wherein themselves excel, in another man
(though absent), whom all know far their inferior in
that faculty; or lastly (to omit other ambushes men
set to surprise praise), when they send the children of
their own brain to be nursed by another man, and
commend their own works in a third person; but, if
challenged by the company that they were authors of
them themselves, with their tongues they faintly deny
it, and with their faces strongly affirm it.

Self-praising comes most naturally from a man when
it comes most violently from him in his own defence.
For though modesty binds a man's tongue to the
peace in this point, yet, being assaulted in his credit,
he may stand upon his guard, and then he doth not
so much praise as purge himself. One braved a
gentleman to his face, that in skill and valour he
came far behind him. 'It is true,' said the other,
'for when I fought with you, you ran away before
me.' In such a case, it was well returned, and without any just aspersion of pride.

He that falls into sin is a man: that grieves at it,
is a saint; that boasteth of it, is a devil. Yet some
glory in their shame, counting the stains of sin the
best complexion for their souls. These men make me
believe it may be true, what Mandeville writes of the
Isle of Somabarre, in the East Indies, that all the

nobility thereof brand their faces with a hot iron, in token of honour.

He that boasts of sins never committed is a double devil. Many brag how many gardens they have deflowered, who never came near the walls thereof. Others (who would sooner creep into a scabbard than draw a sword) boast of their robberies, to usurp the esteem of valour: whereas first let them be well whipped for their lying, and, as they like that, let them come afterward and entitle themselves to the gallows.

OF COMPANY.

COMPANY is one of the greatest pleasures of the nature of man. For the beams of joy are made hotter by reflexion, when related to another; and, otherwise, gladness itself must grieve for want of one to express itself to.

It is unnatural for a man to court and hug solitariness. It is observed, that the farthest islands in the world are so seated that there is none so remote but that, from some shore of it, another island or continent may be discerned; as if hereby nature invited countries to a mutual commerce one with another. Why then should any man affect to environ himself with so deep and great reservedness, as not to communicate with the society of others? And though we pity those who made solitariness their refuge in time of persecution, we must condemn such as choose it in the Church's prosperity. For, well may we count him not well in his wits, who will live always under a bush, because others in a storm shelter themselves under it.

Yet a desert is better than a debauched companion. For the wildness of the place is but. uncheerful; whilst the wildness of bad persons is also infectious. Better, therefore, ride alone, than have a thief's company: and such is a wicked man, who will rob thee of precious time, if he doth no more mischief. The Nazarites, who might drink no wine, were also forbidden to eat grapes (Numb. vi. 3), whereof wine is made. We must not only avoid sin itself, but also the causes and occasions thereof; amongst which, bad company (the lime-twigs of the devil) is the chiefest, especially to catch those natures which, like the good-fellow planet Mercury, are most swayed by others.

If thou beest cast into bad company, like Hercules thou must sleep with thy club in thine hand, and stand on thy guard. I mean, if against thy will the tempest of an unexpected occasion drives thee amongst such rocks; then be thou like the river Dee, in Merionethshire in Wales, which, running through Pimble-mere, remains entire, and mingles not her streams with the waters of the lake. Though with them, be not of them; keep civil communion with them, but separate from their sins. And if against thy will thou fallest amongst wicked men, know to thy comfort, thou art still in thy calling, and therefore in God's keeping, who on thy prayers will preserve thee.

The company he keeps is the comment by help whereof men expound the most close and mystical

man: understanding him for one of the same religion,
life, and manners with his associates. And though
perchance he be not such an one, it is just he should
be counted so for conversing with them.

'He that eat cherries with noblemen shall have his
eyes spirted out with the stones.' This outlandish
proverb hath in it an English truth, that they who
constantly converse with men far above their estates
shall reap shame and loss thereby. If thou payest
nothing, they will count thee a sucker, no branch; a
wen, no member of their company. If in payments
thou keepest pace with them, their long strides will
soon tire thy short legs. The beavers in New England, when some ten of them together draw a stick to
the building of their lodging, set the weakest beavers
to the lighter end of the log, and the strongest take
the heaviest part thereof: whereas men often lay the
greatest burden on the weakest back; and great
persons, to teach meaner men to learn their distance,
take pleasure to make them pay for their company.
I except such men, who, having some excellent
quality, are gratis very welcome to their betters;
such an one, though he pays not a penny of the
shot, spends enough in lending them his time and
discourse.

To affect always to be the best of the company
argues a base disposition. Gold always worn in the
same purse with silver, loses both of the colour and
weight; and so, to converse always with inferiors,
degrades a man of his worth. Such there are that
love to be the lords of the company, whilst the rest
must be their tenants; as if bound by their lease to

approve, praise, and admire whatsoever they say. These, knowing the lowness of their parts, love to live with dwarfs, that they may seem proper men.

It is excellent for one to have a library of scholars, especially if they be plain to be read. I mean, of a communicative nature, whose discourses are as full as fluent, and their judgments as right as their tongues ready: such men's talk shall be thy lectures. To conclude: Good company is not only profitable whilst a man lives, but sometimes when he is dead. For he that was buried with the bones of Elisha, by a posthumous miracle of that prophet, recovered his life by lodging with such a grave-fellow (2 Kings xiii. 21).

OF APPAREL.

CLOTHES are for necessity; warm clothes, for health; cleanly, for decency; lasting, for thrift; and rich, for magnificence. Now there may be a fault in their—number, if too various—making, if too vain—matter, if too costly—and mind of the wearer, if he takes pride therein. We come therefore to some general directions.

It is a chargeable vanity to be constantly clothed above one's purse or place. I say 'constantly;' for, perchance, sometimes it may be dispensed with. A great man, who himself was very plain in apparel, checked a gentleman for being over-fine; who modestly answered, 'Your lordship hath better clothes at home, and I have worse.' But, what shall we say to the riot of our age? wherein (as peacocks are more gay than the eagle himself) subjects are grown braver than their sovereign.

It is beneath a wise man always to wear clothes beneath men of rank. True, there is a state sometimes in decent plainness. When a wealthy lord, at a great solemnity, had the plainest apparel, 'Oh!' said one, 'if you had marked it well, his suit had the richest pockets.' Yet it argues no wisdom, in clothes, always to stoop beneath his condition. When Antisthenes saw Socrates in a torn coat, he showed a hole thereof to the people; 'And, lo!' quoth he, 'through this I see Socrates' pride!'

He shows a light gravity who loves to be an exception from a general fashion. For the received custom in the place where we live is the most competent judge of decency; from which we must not appeal to our own opinion. When the French courtiers, mourning for their King Henry II., had worn cloth a whole year, all silks became so vile in every man's eyes, that if any was seen to wear them, he was presently accounted a mechanic or country-fellow.

It is a folly for one, Proteus-like, never to appear twice in one shape. Had some of our gallants been with the Israelites in the wilderness, when for forty years their clothes waxed not old (Deut. xxix. 5), they would have been vexed, though their clothes were whole, to have been so long in one fashion.

He that is proud of the rustling of his silks, like a madman, laughs at the rattling of his fetters. For indeed, clothes ought to be our remembrancers of our lost innocency. Besides, why should any brag of what is but borrowed? Should the ostrich snatch off the gallant's feather, the beaver his hat, the goat his gloves, the sheep his suit, the silkworm his stockings, and oxen his shoes (to strip him no further than modesty will give leave), he would be left in a cold condition. And yet it is more pardonable to be proud, even of cleanly rags, than, as many are, of affected slovenliness. The one is proud of a molehill, the other of a dunghill.

OF ANGER.

ANGER is one of the sinews of the soul: he that wants it hath a maimed mind, and, with Jacob, sinew-shrunk in the hollow of his thigh, must needs halt. Nor is it good to converse with such as cannot be angry, and, with the Caspian Sea, never ebb nor flow. This anger is either heavenly, when one is offended for God; or hellish, when offended with God and goodness; or earthly, in temporal matters. Which earthly anger (whereof we treat) may also be hellish, if for no cause, no great cause, too hot, or too long.

Be not angry with any without a cause. If thou beest, thou must not only, as the proverb saith, be appeased without amends, having neither cost nor damage given thee, but, as our Saviour saith, be in danger of the judgment (Matt. v. 22).

Be not mortally angry with any for a venial fault. He will make a strange combustion in the state of his soul, who, at the landing of every cock-boat, sets the beacons on fire. To be angry for every toy, debases the worth of thy anger; for he who will be angry for anything, will be angry for nothing.

Let not thy anger be so hot, but that the most torrid zone thereof may be habitable. Fright not people from thy presence with the terror of thy intolerable impatience. Some men, like a tiled house, are long before they take fire; but once on flame, there is no coming near to quench them.

Take heed of doing irrevocable acts in thy passion. As the revealing of secrets, which makes thee a bankrupt for society ever after. Neither do such things which, done once, are done for ever, so that no bemoaning can amend them. Samson's hair grew again, but not his eyes. Time may restore some losses, others are never to be repaired. Wherefore, in thy rage, make no Persian decree which cannot be reversed or repealed; but rather Polonian laws, which (they say) last but three days. Do not in an instant what an age cannot recompense.

Anger kept till the next morning, with manna, doth putrefy and corrupt. Save that manna corrupted not at all, and anger most of all, kept over the next sabbath (Exod. xvi. 24). St. Paul saith, 'Let not the sun go down on your wrath,' (Ephes. iv. 26); to carry news, to the antipodes in another world, of thy revengeful nature. Yet let us take the apostle's meaning rather than his words,—with all possible speed to depose our passion; not understanding him so literally that we may take leave to be angry till sunset: then might our wrath lengthen with the days; and men in Greenland, where day lasts above a quarter of a year, have plentiful scope of revenge. And as the English, by command from William the Conqueror, always raked up their fire, and put out their candles, when the curfew-bell was rung, let us then also quench all sparks of anger and heat of passion.

He that keeps anger long in his bosom giveth place to the devil (Ephes. iv. 27). And why should we make room for him, who will crowd in too fast of himself? Heat of passion makes our souls to chap, and the devil creeps in at the crannies; yea, a furious man in his fits may seem possessed with a devil, foams, fumes, tears himself; is deaf and dumb, in effect, to hear or speak reason; sometimes wallows, stares, stamps, with fiery eyes and flaming cheeks. Had Narcissus himself seen his own face when he had been angry, he could never have fallen in love with himself.

OF CONTENTMENT.

It is one property which (they say) is required of those who seek for the philosopher's stone, that they must not do it with any covetous desire to be rich; for otherwise they shall never find it. But most true it is, that whosoever would have this jewel of contentment (which turns all into gold, yea, want into wealth) must come with minds divested of all ambitious and covetous thoughts, else are they never likely to obtain it. We will describe contentment first negatively:—

It is not a senseless stupidity respecting what becomes of our outward estates. God would have us take notice of all accidents, which, from him, happen to us in worldly matters. Had the martyrs had the dead palsy before they went to the stake to be burnt, their sufferings had not been so glorious.

It is not a word-braving or scorning of all wealth in discourse. Generally those who boast most of contentment have least of it. Their very boasting shows that they want something, and basely beg it, namely, commendation. These in their language are like unto kites in their flying, which mount in the air so scornfully, as if they disdained to stoop for the whole earth, fetching about many stately circuits. But what is the spirit these conjurers, with so many circles, intend to raise? A poor chicken, or, perchance, a piece of carrion: and so the height of the others' proud boasting will humble itself for a little base gain.

But it is a humble and willing submitting ourselves to God's pleasure in all conditions. One observeth (how truly, I dispute not!) that the French naturally have so elegant and graceful a carriage, that what posture of body soever in their salutations, or what fashion of attire soever they are pleased to take on them, it doth so beseem them that one would think nothing can become them better. Thus, contentment makes men carry themselves gracefully in wealth, want, health, sickness, freedom, fetters, yea, what condition soever God allots them.

It is no breach of contentment for men to complain that their sufferings are unjust, as offered by men—provided they allow them for just, as proceeding from God, who useth wicked men's injustice to correct his children. But let us take heed that we bite not so high at the handle of the rod as to fasten on His hand that holds it; our discontentments mounting so high, as to quarrel with God himself.

It is no breach of contentment for men, by lawful

means, to seek the removal of their misery, and better-
ing of their estate. Thus men ought, by industry, to
endeavour the getting of more wealth, ever submitting
themselves to God's will. A lazy hand is no argument of a contented heart. Indeed, he that is idle,
and followeth after vain persons, shall have enough:
but how? 'Shall have poverty enough' (Prov.
xxviii. 19).

God's Spirit is the best schoolmaster to teach
contentment: a schoolmaster who can make good
scholars, and warrant the success as well as his endeavour. The school of sanctified afflictions is the
best place to learn contentment in: I say 'sanctified;' for, naturally, like resty horses, we go the
worse for the beating, if God bless not afflictions
unto us.

Contentment consisteth not in adding more fuel,
but in taking away some fire—not in multiplying of
wealth, but in subtracting men's desires. Worldly
riches, like nuts, tear many clothes in getting them,
spoil many teeth in cracking them, but fill no belly
with eating them. Yea, our souls may sooner surfeit
than be satisfied with earthly things. He that at
first thought ten thousand pounds too much for any
one man, will afterwards think ten millions too little
for himself.

Pious meditations much advantage contentment in
adversity. Such as these are, to consider: First, that
more are beneath us than above us. Secondly, many
of God's dear saints have been in the same condition.
Thirdly, we want rather superfluities than necessaries.
Fourthly, the more we have, the more we must ac-

count for. Fifthly, earthly blessings, through man's corruption, are more prone to be abused than well-used. In some fenny places in England, where they are much troubled with gnats, they used to hang up dung in the midst of the room for a bait for the gnats to fly to, and so catch them with a net provided for the purpose. Thus the devil ensnareth the souls of many men by illuring[1] them with the muck and dung of this world, to undo them eternally. Sixthly, we must leave all earthly wealth at our death; 'and riches avail not in the day of wrath.' But as some used to fill up the stamp of light gold with dirt, thereby to make it weigh the heavier; so it seems some men load their souls with thick clay, to make them pass the better in God's balance: but all to no purpose. Seventhly, the less we have, the less it will grieve us to leave this world. Lastly, it is the will of God, and therefore both for his glory and our good, whereof we ought to be assured. I have heard how a gentleman, travelling in a misty morning, asked of a shepherd (such men being generally skilled in the physiognomy of the heavens) what weather it would be. 'It will be,' said the shepherd, 'what weather shall please me:' and being courteously requested to express his meaning; 'Sir,' said he, 'it shall be what weather pleaseth God; and what weather pleaseth God, pleaseth me.' Thus contentment maketh men to have what they think fitting themselves, because submitting to God's will and pleasure.

To conclude: A man ought to be like a cunning

---

[1] Deceiving, beguiling. Illusion and illusive, from the same root, still remain in use.

actor, who, if he be enjoined to represent the perso of some prince or nobleman, does it with a grace and comeliness; if, by-and-by, he be commanded to lay that aside and play the beggar, he does that as willingly and as well.

OF TIME-SERVING.

THERE be four kinds of time-serving. First, out of Christian discretion, which is commendable. Second, out of human infirmity, which is more pardonable. Third and fourth, out of ignorance or affectation, both which are damnable. Of them in order :—

He is a good time-server that complies his manners to the several ages of this life. Pleasant in youth, without wantonness; grave in old age, without frowardness. Frost is as proper for winter as flowers for spring. Gravity becomes the ancient; and a green Christmas is neither handsome nor healthful.

He is a good time-server that finds out the fittest opportunity for every action. God hath made 'a time for everything under the sun,' save only for that which we do at all times,—to wit, sin.

He is a good time-server that improves the present for God's glory and his own salvation. Of all the extent of time, only the instant is that we can call 'ours.'

He is a good time-server that is pliant to the times in matters of mere indifferency. To blame are they whose minds may seem to be made of one entire bone, without any joints. They cannot bend at all, but stand as stiffly in things of pure indifferency as in matters of absolute necessity.

He is a good time-server that in time of persecution neither betrays God's cause nor his own safety. And this he may do,—

1. By lying hid both in his person and practice. Though he will do no evil, he will forbear the public doing of some good. He hath as good cheer in his heart, though he keeps not open house, and will not publicly broach his religion, till the palate of the times be better in taste to relish it. 'The prudent shall keep silence in that time, for it is an evil time' (Amos v. 13); though, according to St. Peter's command, we are 'to give a reason of our hope to every one that asketh' (1 Peter iii. 15); namely, that asketh for his instruction, but not for our destruction, especially if wanting lawful authority to examine us. 'Ye shall be brought,' saith Christ (no need have they, therefore, to run!), 'before governors and kings for my sake' (Matt. x. 18).

2. By flying away. If there be no absolute necessity of his staying, no scandal given by his flight; if he wants strength to stay it out till death; and, lastly, if God openeth a fair way for his departure. Otherwise, if God bolts the doors and windows against him, he is not to creep out at the top of the chimney, and escape by unwarrantable courses. If all should fly, truth would want champions for the present; if none should fly, truth might want champions for the future.

We come now to time-servers out of infirmity:—

Heart-of-oak hath sometimes warped a little in the

F

scorching heat of persecution. Their want of true courage herein cannot be excused. Yet many censure them for surrendering up their forts after a long siege, who would have yielded up their own at the first summons. Oh! there is more required to make one valiant, than to call Cranmer or Jewel 'coward;' as if the fire in Smithfield had been no hotter than what is painted in the *Book of Martyrs.*

Yet afterwards they have come into their former straightness and stiffness. The troops which at first rather wheeled about than ran away, have come in seasonable at last. Yea, their constant blushing for shame of their former cowardliness hath made their souls ever after look more modest and beautiful. Thus Cranmer, who subscribed to Popery, grew valiant afterwards, and thrust his right hand, which subscribed, first into the fire; so that *that* hand died (as it were) a malefactor, and all the rest of his body a martyr.

Some have served the times out of mere ignorance. Gaping, for company, as others gaped before them, *Pater noster*, or 'Our Father.'[1] I could both sigh and smile at the witty simplicity of a poor old woman, who had lived in the days of Queen Mary and Queen Elizabeth, and said her prayers daily both in Latin and English; and 'Let God,' said she, 'take to himself which he likes best.'

But worst are those who serve the times out of mere affectation. Doing as the times do, not because the times do as they should do, but merely for sinister

[1] The Lord's prayer, either according to the Popish or Protestant form.

respects, to ingratiate themselves. We read of an earl of Oxford fined by King Henry VII. fifteen thousand marks for having too many retainers. But how many retainers hath time had in all ages, and servants in all offices! yea, and chaplains too!

Time-servers are oftentimes left in the lurch. Such, when the times turn afterwards to another extreme, are left in the briers, and come off very hardly from the bill of their hands. If they turn again with the times, none will trust them; for who will make a staff of an osier?

Miserable will be the condition of such time-servers when their master is taken from them—when, as the angel swore, that 'TIME shall be no longer' (Rev. x. 6). Therefore, it is best serving of Him who is ETERNITY, a Master that can ever protect us.

To conclude: He that intends to meet with one in a great fair, and knows not where he is, may sooner find him by standing still in some principal place there, than by traversing it up and down. Take thy stand on some good ground in religion, and keep thy station in a fixed posture, never hunting after the times to follow them; and, a hundred to one, they will come to thee once in thy life-time.

THE WITCH OF ENDOR.

(1 Sam. xxviii.)

HER proper name we neither find, nor need curiously inquire; without it, she is described enough for our knowledge, too much for her shame.

King Saul had banished all witches and sorcerers

out of Israel; but no besom can sweep so clean as to leave no crumb of dust behind it. This witch of Endor still keeps herself safe in the land. God hath 'his remnant,' where saints are cruelly persecuted; Satan also his remnant, where offenders are severely prosecuted, and (if there were no more) the whole species of witches is preserved in this *individuum*, till more be provided.

It happened now, that King Saul, being ready to fight with the Philistines, was in great distress, because God answered him not concerning the success· of the battle. With the silent, He will be silent: Saul gave no real answer in his obedience to God's commands, God will give no vocal answer to Saul's requests.

Men's minds are naturally ambitious to know things to come: Saul is restless to know the issue of the fight. Alas! what needed he to set his teeth on edge with the sourness of that bad tidings, who soon after was to have his belly full thereof?

He said to his servants, 'Seek me out' (no wonder she was such a jewel to be sought for!) 'one with a familiar spirit.' Which was accordingly performed, and Saul came to her in a disguise. Formerly Samuel told him that his 'disobedience was as witchcraft;' now Saul falls from the like to the same, and tradeth with witches indeed (the receiver is as bad as the thief!), and at his request she raiseth up Samuel to come unto him.

'What! true Samuel?' It is above Satan's power to degrade a saint from glory, though for a moment: since his own fall thence he could fetch none from

heaven. 'Or was it only the true body of Samuel?'
No; the precious ashes of the saints (the pawn for
the return of their souls!) are locked up safe in the
cabinet of their graves, and the devil hath no key
unto it.

. 'Or, 'lastly, was it his seeming body?' He that
could not counterfeit the least and worst of worms
(Exod. viii. 18), could he dissemble the shape of one
of the best and greatest of men? Yet this is most
probable, seeing Satan could change himself into an
angel of light, and God gives him more power at some
times than at other. However, we will not be too
peremptory herein, and build standing structures of
bold assertions on so uncertain a foundation : rather,
with the Rechabites, we will live in tents of conjectures, which, on better reason, we may easily alter
and remove.

The devil's speech looks backward and forward,
relates and foretells. The historical part thereof is
easy, recounting God's special favours to Saul, and
his ingratitude to God, and the matter thereof very
pious. 'Not every one that saith, Lord, Lord!'
(whether *to* him or *of* him!) 'shall enter into the
kingdom of heaven.' For Satan here useth the
Lord's name six times in four verses. The prophetical
part of his speech is harder, how he could foretell,
'To-morrow shalt thou and thy sons be with me.'
'What! with me, true Samuel, in heaven?' That
was too good a place (will some say) for Saul. 'Or
with me, true Satan, in hell?' That was too bad a
place for Jonathan. 'What then?' 'With me, pretended Samuel, in hades, in the state of the dead.'

But how came the witch or Satan by this knowledge? Surely that ugly monster never looked his face in that beautiful glass of the Trinity, which (as some will have it) represents things to the blessed angels. No doubt, then, he gathered it by experimental collection, who, having kept an exact ephemerides of all actions for more than five thousand years together, can thereby make a more than probable guess of future contingents; the rather, because accidents in this world are not so much new as renewed. Besides, he saw it in the natural causes,— in the strength of the Philistines and weakness of the Israelitish army, and in David's ripeness to succeed Saul in the throne. Perchance, as vultures are said to smell the earthliness of a dying corpse; so this bird of prey resented a worse than earthly savour in the soul of Saul,—an evidence of his death at hand. Or else we may say, the devil knew it by particular revelation; for God, to use the devil for his own turn, might impart it unto him, to advance wicked men's repute of Satan's power, that they who *would* be deceived *should* be deceived to believe that Satan knows more than he does.

The dismal news so frighted Saul, that he fell along on the earth; and yet at last is persuaded to arise and eat meat, she killing and dressing a fat calf for him.

Witches generally are so poor they can scarce feed themselves. See here one able to feast a king. ' That which goeth into the mouth defileth not.' Better eat meat of her dressing, than take counsel of her giving; and her hands might be clean, whose soul meddled with unclean spirits. Saul must eat somewhat, that he might be strengthened to live to be killed, as afterwards it came to pass. And here the mention of this witch in Scripture vanisheth away, and we will follow her no further. If afterwards she escaped the justice of man, God's judgment, without her repentance, hath long since overtaken her.

THE ATHEIST.

THE word 'atheist' is of a very large extent: every polytheist is, in effect, an atheist; for he that multiplies a deity, annihilates it : and he that divides it, destroys it.

But, amongst the heathen, we may observe that whosoever sought to withdraw people from their idolatry was presently indicted and arraigned of atheism. If any philosopher saw God through their gods, this dust was cast in his eyes for being more quick-sighted than others, that presently he was condemned for an atheist; and thus Socrates, the Pagan martyr, was put to death as an atheist. At this day three sorts of atheists are extant in the world :—

1. In life and conversation.—'God is not in all his thoughts' (Psalm x. 4): not that he thinks there is no God; but he thinks not there is a God, never minding or heeding Him in the whole course of his life and actions.

2. In will and desire.—Such could wish there were

no God nor devil; as thieves would have no judge nor jailor. *Quod metuunt periisse expetunt.*[1]

3. In judgment and opinion.—Of the former two sorts of atheists, there are more in the world than are generally thought; of this latter, more are thought to be than there-are;—a contemplative atheist being very rare, such as were Diagoras, Protagoras, Lucian, and Theodorus, who, though carrying God in his name, was an atheist in his opinion.

Come we to see by what degrees a man may climb up to this height of profaneness. And we will suppose him to be one living in wealth and prosperity, which more disposeth men to atheism than adversity. For, affliction mindeth men of a Deity, as those who are pinched will cry, 'O Lord!' But much outward happiness, abused, occasioneth men, as wise Agur observeth, 'to deny God, and say, "Who is the Lord?"'

First, he quarrels at the diversities of religions in the world,—complaining how great clerks dissent in their judgments, which makes him sceptical in all opinions: whereas such differences should not make men careless to have any, but careful to have the best, religion.

He loveth to maintain paradoxes, and to shut his eyes against the beams of a known truth. Not only for discourse, which might be permitted: for as no cloth can be woven except the woof and the warp be cast cross one to another, so discourse will not be maintained without some opposition for the time. But our inclining atheist goes farther, engaging his

---

[1] 'They wish the destruction of that which they dread.'

affections in disputes, even in such matters where the supposing them wounds piety, but the positive maintaining them stabs it to the heart.

He scoffs and makes sport at sacred things. This, by degrees, abates the reverence of religion, and ulcers men's hearts with profaneness. The Popish proverb, well understood, hath a truth in it : ' Never dog barked against the crucifix, but he ran mad.'

Hence he proceeds to take exception at God's word. He keeps a register of many difficult places of Scripture ; not that he desires satisfaction therein, but delights to puzzle divines therewith ; and counts it a great conquest when he hath posed them. Unnecessary questions out of the Bible are his most necessary study ; and he is more curious to know where Lazarus's soul was, the four days he lay in the grave, than careful to provide for his own soul when he shall be dead. Thus is it just with God, that they who will not feed on the plain meat of his word, should be choked with the bones thereof. But his principal delight is to sound the alarum, and to set several places of Scripture to fight one against another, betwixt which there is a seeming, and he would make a real, contradiction.

Afterwards he grows so impudent as to deny the Scripture itself. As Samson, being fastened by a web to a pin, carried away both web and pin ; so if any urge our atheist with arguments from Scripture, and tie him to the authority of God's word, he denies both reason and God's word, to which the reason is fastened.

Hence he proceeds to deny God himself. First, in

his administration ; then, in his essence. What else could be expected but that he should bite at last who had snarled so long ? First, he denies God's ordering of sublunary matters. 'Tush, doth the Lord see, or is there knowledge in the Most High ?' making him a maimed Deity, without an eye of providence or an arm of power, and, at most, restraining him only to matters above the clouds. But he that dares to confine the King of heaven, will soon after endeavour to depose him, and fall, at last, flatly to deny him.

He furnisheth himself with an armoury of arguments to fight against his own conscience. Some taken from—

1. The impunity and outward happiness of wicked men. And no wonder if an atheist breaks his neck thereat, whereat the foot of David himself did almost slip when he saw the prosperity of the wicked (Psalm lxxiii. 2, 3): whom God only reprieves for punishment hereafter.

2. From the afflictions of the godly, whilst, indeed, God only tries their faith by patience. As Absalom complained of his father David's government, that none were deputed to redress people's grievances; so he objects that none righteth the wrongs of God's people, and thinks (proud dust !) the world would be better steered if he were the pilot thereof.

3. From the delaying of the day of judgment, with those mockers whose objections the apostle fully answereth (2 Peter iii.). And in regard of his own particular, the atheist hath as little cause to rejoice at the deferring of the day of judgment, as the thief hath reason to be glad that the assizes be

put off, who is to be tried, and may be executed before, at the quarter-sessions : so death may take our atheist off, before the day of judgment come.

With these and other arguments he struggles with his own conscience, and long in vain seeks to conquer it, even fearing that Deity he flouts at, and dreading that God whom he denies. And as that famous Athenian soldier, Cynægirus, catching hold of one of the enemy's ships, held it first with his right hand, and, when that was cut off, with his left, and when both were cut off, yet still kept it with his teeth ; so the conscience of our atheist—though he bruise it, and beat it, and maim it never so much—still keeps him by the teeth, still feeding and gnawing upon him, torturing and tormenting him with thoughts of a Deity which the other desires to suppress.

At last he himself is utterly overthrown by conquering his own conscience. God in justice takes from him the light which he thrust from himself, and delivers him up to a seared conscience and a reprobate mind, whereby hell takes possession of him. The apostle saith that a man may feel God in his works (Acts xvii. 27). But our atheist hath a dead palsy, is past all sense, and cannot perceive God, who is everywhere presented to him.

THE HERETIC.

IT is very difficult accurately to define him. Amongst the heathen atheist was, and amongst Christians heretic is, the disgraceful word-of-course, always cast upon those who dissent from the predominant current of the time. Thus those who in matters of opinion varied from the Pope's copy the least hair-stroke, are condemned for heretics. Yea, Virgilius, Bishop of Saltzburg, was branded with that censure, for maintaining that there were antipodes opposite to the then known world. It may be, as Alexander, hearing the philosophers dispute of more worlds, wept that he had conquered no part of them; so it grieved the Pope that these antipodes were not subject to his jurisdiction, which much incensed his holiness against the strange opinion. We will branch the description of a heretic into these three parts:

1. He is one that formerly hath been of the true Church. 'They went out from us, but they were not of us' (1 John ii. 19). These afterwards prove more offensive to the Church than very Pagans; as the English-Irish, descended anciently of English parentage, (be it spoken with the more shame to them, and sorrow to us!) turning wild, become worse enemies to our nation than the native Irish themselves.

2. Maintaining a fundamental error. Every scratch in the hand is not a stab to the heart; nor doth every false opinion make a heretic.

3. With obstinacy. Which is the dead flesh, making the green wound of an error fester into the old sore of a heresy.

It matters not much what manner of person he hath. If beautiful, perchance the more attractive of feminine followers: if deformed, so that his body is as odd as his opinions, he is the more properly entitled to the reputation of 'crooked saint.'

His natural parts are quick and able. Yet he that shall ride on a winged horse to tell him thereof, shall but come too late, to bring him stale news of what he knew too well before.

Learning is necessary in him, if he trades in a critical error. But if he only broaches dregs, and deals in some dull, sottish opinion, a trowel will serve as well as a pencil to daub on such thick coarse colours. Yea, in some heresies, deep studying is so useless, that the first thing they learn is to inveigh against all learning.

However, some smattering in the original tongues will do well. On occasion, he will let fly whole volleys of Greek and Hebrew words; whereby he not only amazeth his ignorant auditors, but also in conference daunteth many of his opposers, who, though in all other learning far his superiors, may perchance be conscious of want of skill in those languages, whilst the heretic hereby gains credit to his cause and person.

His behaviour is seemingly very pious and devout. How foul soever the postern and back-door be, the gate opening to the street is swept and garnished, and his outside adorned with pretended austerity.

He is extremely proud, and discontented with the times—quarrelling that many, beneath him in piety, are above him in place. This pride hath caused many men who otherwise might have been 'shining lights,' to prove smoking firebrands in the Church.

Having first hammered the heresy in himself, he then falls to seducing of others. So hard is it for one to have the itch, and not to scratch. Yea, Babylon herself will allege, that ' for Sion's sake she will not hold her peace.' The necessity of propagating the truth is error's plea to divulge her falsehoods. Men, as naturally they desire to know, so they desire what they know should be known.

If challenged to a private dispute, his impudence bears him out. He counts it the only error, to confess he hath erred. His face is of brass, which may be said either ever or never to blush. In disputing, his *modus* is *sine modo*;[1] and, as if all figures (even in logic) were magical, he neglects all forms of reasoning, counting *that* the only syllogism *which* is his conclusion.

He slights any synod, if condemning his opinions. Esteeming the decisions thereof no more than the forfeits in a barber's shop, where a gentleman's pleasure is all the obligation to pay, and none are bound except they will bind themselves.

[1] ' His method is immethodical.'

MISCELLANEOUS EXTRACTS.

FULLER was a most prolific and voluminous writer. A mere list of the titles of his published works would fill several pages; to give selections from them all would be impossible. The names of the most important have been recorded, and the circumstances under which they were written narrated in the Memoir prefixed to this volume. The extracts which follow are taken from his *Church History of Britain*, his *Worthies of England*, and from Sermons, Expositions, and other minor treatises. The passages selected from his historical works will illustrate the quaint, humorous, anecdotical manner in which he wrote even Ecclesiastical history.

Primitive Monks.—When the furnace of persecution in the infancy of Christianity was grown so hot, that most cities, towns, and populous places were visited with that epidemical disease, many pious men fled into deserts, there to live with more safety, and serve God with less disturbance. No wild humour to make themselves miserable, and to choose and court their own calamity, put them on this project; much less any superstitious opinion of transcendent sanctity in a solitary life made them willingly to leave their former habitations. For, whereas all men by their birth are indebted to their country, there to stay and discharge all civil relations, it had been dishonesty in them, like bankrupts, to run away into the wilderness to defraud their country, their creditor, except some violent occasion (such as persecution was) forced them thereunto : and this was the first original of monks in the world, so called from μόνος, because 'living alone by themselves.'

Here they, in the deserts, hoped to find rocks and stocks, yea, beasts themselves, more kind than men had been to them. What would hide and heat, cover and keep warm, served them for clothes, not placing (as their successors in after-ages) any holiness in their habits, folded up in the affected fashion thereof. As for their food, the grass was their cloth, the ground their table, herbs and roots their diet, wild fruits and berries their dainties, hunger their sauce, their nails their knives, their hands their cups, the next well their wine-cellar. But what their bill-of-fare wanted in cheer, it had in grace; their life being constantly spent in prayer, reading, musing, and such-like pious employments. They turned solitariness itself into society; and, cleaving themselves asunder by the divine art of meditation, did make, of one, two or more, opposing, answering, moderating in their own bosoms, and busying themselves with variety of heavenly recreations. It would do one good even but to think of their goodness, and at the re-bound and second-hand to meditate on their meditations. For if ever poverty was to be envied, it was here. And I appeal to the moderate men of these times, whether, in the height of those woful wars, they have not sometimes wished (not out of passionate distemper, but serious recollection of themselves) some such private place to retire unto, where, out of the noise of this clamorous world, they might have reposed themselves, and served God with more quiet.

These monks were of two sorts, either such as fled from actual, or from imminent persecution. For when a danger is not created by a timorous fancy, but rationally represented as probable, in such a case the principles of prudence, not out of cowardice but caution, warrant men to provide for their safety. Neither of these bound themselves with a wilful vow to observe poverty, but poverty rather vowed to observe them, waiting constantly upon them. Neither did they vow chastity, though keeping it better than such as vowed it in after-ages. As for the vow of obedience, it was both needless and impossible in their condition, having none beneath or above them ; living alone, and their whole convent, as one may say, consisting of a single person. And as they entered on this course of life rather by impulsion than election, so when peace was restored, they returned to their former homes in cities and towns, resuming their callings, which they had not left off, but for a time laid aside.

Miracles at the Tomb of St. Chad and Thomas à Becket.—St. Chad, in Latin *Cedda*, born in Northumberland, bred likewise in Holy Island, and scholar to Aidanus. He was bishop of Lichfield ; a mild and modest man, of whom more hereafter. His death is celebrated in the Calendar, March 2nd, and the dust of his tomb is by Papists reported to cure all diseases alike in man and beast. I believe it might make *the dumb to see, and the lame to speak*.

*   *   *

And now being on this subject, once to despatch Becket out of our way, just a jubilee of years after his death, Stephen Langton, his mediate successor, removed his body from the Under-croft in Christchurch, where first he was buried, and laid him, at his own charge, in a most sumptuous shrine, at the east end of the church. Here the rust of the sword that killed him was afterwards tendered to pilgrims to kiss. Here many miracles were pretended to be wrought by this saint, in number two hundred and seventy. They might well have been brought up to four hundred, and made as many as Baal's lying

prophets ; though, even then, one prophet of the
Lord, one Micaiah, one true miracle, were worth
them all.

Gustavus Adolphus on the Jesuits.—The
very Jesuits themselves tasted of his courtesy,
though merrily he laid it to their charge, that they
would neither *preach faith* to, nor *keep faith* with,
others.

The fatal vespers at Blackfriars.—Now happened the sad vespers, or doleful even-song, at Blackfriars, in London, October 26th (1623).   Father
Drury, a Jesuit of excellent morals and ingratiating
converse (wanting nothing, saving the embracing of
the truth, to make him valuable in himself and
acceptable to others), preached in a great upper room
in Blackfriars, next to the house of the French
ambassador, where some three hundred persons were
assembled.   His text, 'O thou ungracious servant!
I forgave thee all the debt, because thou desiredst
me ; shouldst not thou also have had compassion on
thy fellow-servant ?'   In application whereof, he fell
upon a bitter invective against the Protestants.

His sermon began to incline to the middle, the day
to the end, thereof; when on the sudden the floor
fell down whereon they were assembled.   It gave no
charitable warning groan beforehand, but cracked,
brake, and fell, all in an instant.   Many were killed,
more bruised, all frighted. Sad sight to behold the flesh
and blood of different persons mingled together, and
the brains of one on the head of another !   One
lacked a leg ; another, an arm ; a third, whole and
entire, wanting nothing but breath, stifled in the

ruins. Some Protestants, coming merely to see, were made to suffer, and bear the heavy burden of their own curiosity. About ninety-five persons were slain outright ; amongst whom Mr. Drury and Mr. Rodiat, priests, with the lady Webbe, were of the greatest quality.

All the Martyrs not alike cheerful.—All who met at last in final constancy manifested not equal intermediate cheerfulness. Some were more stout, bold, and resolute ; others more faint, fearful, and timorous. Of the latter was Archbishop Cranmer, who first subscribed a recantation, but afterwards recanted his subscription, and valiantly burned at the stake. Thus, he that stumbleth, and doth not fall down, gaineth ground thereby ; as this good man's slip mended his pace to his martyrdom.

It is also observable that married people, the parents of many children, suffered death with most alacrity : Mr. Rogers and Dr. Taylor may be the instances thereof. The former of these, if consulting with flesh and blood, had eleven strong reasons to favour himself ; I mean a wife and ten children : all which abated not his resolution.

Besides these, who were put to death, some scores (not to say hundreds) died, or rather were killed, with stench, starving, and strait usage in prison. I am not satisfied in what distance properly to place these persons. Some, perchance, will account it too high to rank them amongst martyrs ; and, surely, I conceive it too low to esteem them but bare confessors. The best is, the heraldry of Heaven knows how to marshal them in the place of dignity due unto them ;

where, long since, they have received the reward of their patience.

Wickliffe's ashes burned and drowned.— Hitherto the corpse of John Wickliffe had quietly slept in his grave, about one-and-forty years after his death, till his body was reduced to bones, and his bones almost to dust.   For though the earth in the chancel of Lutterworth, where he was interred, had not so quick a digestion with the earth of Aceldama, yet such the appetite thereof, and all other English graves, to leave small reversions of a body after so many years.

But now, such the spleen of the Council of Constance, as they not only cursed his memory, as dying an obstinate heretic, but ordered his bones (with this charitable caution, ' if it may be discerned from the bodies of other faithful people ') to be taken out of the ground, and thrown far off from any Christian burial.

In obedience hereunto, Richard Fleming sent his officers (vultures with a quick sight and scent at a dead carcase!) to ungrave him accordingly.   To Lutterworth they come, — sumner, commissary, official, chancellor, proctors, doctors, and the servants (so that the remnant of the body would not hold out a bone, amongst so many hands) take what was left out of the grave, and burnt them to ashes, and cast them into Swift, a neighbouring brook running hard by.   Thus this brook hath conveyed his ashes into Avon, Avon into Severn, Seven into the narrow seas, they into the main ocean.   And thus the ashes of Wickliffe are the emblem of his doctrine, which is now dispersed all the world over.

Christian Perfection.—In a fourfold respect may a servant of God be pronounced perfect in this life :

1. Comparatively, in reference to wicked men, who have not the least degree or desire of goodness in them. Measure a servant of God by such a dwarf, and he will seem a proper person, yea, comparatively perfect.

2. Intentionally : the drift, scope, and purpose of such a man's life is to desire perfection, which desires are seconded with all the strength of his weak endeavours. He draweth his bow with all his might, and perfection is the mark he aimeth at, though too often his hand shakes, his bow starts, and his arrow misses.

3. Inchoatively : we have here the beginning and the earnest as of the Spirit (2 Cor. i. 22). So of all spiritual graces, expecting the full (not payment, because a mere gift, but) receipt of the rest hereafter. In this world we are a-perfecting, and in the next (Heb. xii. 23) we shall come to the spirits of just men made perfect.

But blame me not, beloved, if I be brief in these three kinds of perfections, rather touching than landing at them, in our discourse; seeing I am partly afraid, partly ashamed, to lay too much stress and weight on such slight and slender foundations. I hasten with all convenient speed to the fourth, which one is worth all the rest. A servant of God in this life is perfect :

4. Imputatively : Christ's perfections through God's mercy being imputed unto him. If I be worsted in my front, and beaten in my main battle, I am sure I

can safely retreat to this my invincible rear. In the
agony of temptation we must quit comparative perfection. Alas, relation is rather a shadow than a
substance. Quit intentional perfection, being conscious to ourselves how oft our actions cross our
intentions. Quit inchoative perfection; for whilst a
servant of God compareth the little goodness he hath
with that great proportion which by God's law he
ought to have, he conceiveth thereof as the pious Jews
did of the foundation of the second temple (Hag.
ii. 3): 'Is it not in your eyes in comparison of it as
nothing?' But stick we may and must to imputative
perfection, which indeed is God's act, clothing us with
the righteousness of Jesus Christ.

This is the reason the saints are unwilling to own
any other perfection: for though God is pleased to
style Job 'a perfect man,' yet see what he said of
himself: 'If I say that I am perfect, it shall also
prove me perverse.' God might say it: Job durst
not, for fear of pride and presumption. Indeed, Noah
is the first person who is pronounced perfect in
Scripture. But mark, I pray, what went in the verse
before: 'But Noah found grace in the eyes of the
Lord.' Not that his finding grace is to be confined
to his particular preservation from the deluge (which
was but one branch or sprig of God's grace unto him);
but his whole person was by God's goodness accepted
of; Noah's perfection more consisting in that accept-
ance than his own amiableness; approved not so
much because God found goodness in Noah, but
because Noah found grace in God.

Grace to be held fast in the midst of tem-

poral losses.—As it is with a man in a wreck at sea, when all is cast overboard,—the victuals that feed him, the clothes that should keep him warm,—yet he swims to the shore with his life in his hand ; or as it is with a valiant standard-bearer that carries the banner in the time of battle, if he sees all lost, he wraps the banner about his body, and chooseth rather to die in that as his winding-sheet, than let any man take it from or spoil him of it—he will hold that fast, though he lose his life with it. Thus Job in all his troubles is said to hold fast his integrity. And so must all of us do, hold our spirituals, whatsoever becomes of our temporals. When wife and children, and friends, and liberty, and life, and all is a-going, say unto peace of conscience, to innocency and integrity, as Jacob said to the angel (whether they be those summer-graces of prosperity, as joy and thanksgiving ; or the winter graces of adversity, as patience and perseverance ; or the grace of humility that is always in season), ' We will not let you go :' for indeed there is no blessing without them. There's not a man upon the face of the earth, but, if he be of a heavenly temper and spiritual resolution, will, in the greatest storm, in the hottest assault, wrap himself round about with his integrity, and will not let it go, till he go along with it.   .

The Resurrection.—I have stood in a smith's forge, and seen him put a rusty, cold, dull piece of iron into the fire, and, after awhile, he hath taken the same piece, the very same numerical individual piece of iron out of the fire, but bright, sparkling. And thus it is with our bodies: they are laid down in the grave dead, heavy, earthly; but at the resurrection, this mortal shall put on immortality; at that general conflagration, this dead, heavy, earthly body shall arise living, lightsome, glorious; which made Job so confident; 'I know that my Redeemer liveth, and that with these eyes I shall see him' (xix. 25).

God slow to anger and of great patience.—It is observable that the Roman magistrates, when they gave sentence upon any one to be scourged, a bundle of rods tied hard with many knots was laid before them. The reason was this, that whilst the beadle or flagellifer was untying the knots, which he was to do by [*i.e.* in] order and not in any other hasty or sudden way, the magistrate might see the deportment and carriage of the delinquent, whether he were sorry for his fault and showed any hope of amendment, that then he might recall his sentence or mitigate the punishment; otherwise to be corrected so much the more severely. Thus God in the punishment of sinners, how patient is he! how loth to strike! how slow to anger if there be but any hopes of recovery! How many knots doth he untie! How many rubs doth he make in his way to justice! He doth not try us by martial law, but pleads the case with us, 'Why will ye die, O house of Israel?' and all this to see whether the poor sinner will throw himself down at his feet, whether he will come in and make his composition, and be saved.

Poor professors preserved by God's providence.—God hath always been ambitious to preserve and prefer little things. The Jews—'the least' of all nations; David their king—'least' in his father's family; 'little' Benjamin the ruler; 'little' hill of Hermon; the Virgin Mary—'the lowliness' of thy handmaiden. God's children, severally, are styled his 'little ones,' and collectively make up but a 'little flock.' And, surely, it renders the work of grace more visible and conspicuous, when the object can claim nothing as due to itself. A pregnant proof hereof we have in Divine Providence at this time preserving the inconsiderable pittance of faithful professors against most powerful opposition. This handful of men were tied to very hard duty, being constantly to stand sentinels against an army of enemies, till God sent Luther to relieve them : and the work was made lighter, with more hands to do it.

A pleasant story of King Henry VIII.—King Henry VIII. as he was hunting in Windsor Forest, either casually lost, or (more probable) wilfully losing himself, struck down about dinner-time to the abbey of Reading : where, disguising himself (much for delight, more for discovery, to see unseen), he was invited to the abbot's table, and passed for one of the king's guard, a place to which the proportion of his person might properly entitle him. A sirloin of beef was set before him (so knighted, saith tradition, by this King Henry), on which the king laid on lustily, not disgracing one of that place for whom he was mistaken. 'Well fare thy heart!' quoth the abbot, ' and here, in a cup of sack, I remember the health of his Grace your master. I would give a hundred pounds on the condition I could feed so heartily on beef as you do. Alas! my weak and queasy stomach will hardly digest the wing of a small rabbit or chicken.'

The king pleasantly pledged him, and, heartily thanking him for his good cheer, after dinner departed, as undiscovered as he came thither.

Some weeks after, the abbot was sent for, by a pursuivant, brought up to London, clapped in the Tower, kept close prisoner, fed for a short time with bread and water. Yet not so empty his body of food as his mind was filled with fears, creating many suspicions to himself when and how he had incurred the king's displeasure. At last a sirloin of beef was set before him, on which the abbot fed as the farmer of his grange, and verified the proverb, that 'two hungry meals makes the third a glutton.', In springs King Henry out of a private lobby, where he had placed himself, the invisible spectator of the abbot's behaviour. 'My lord,' quoth the king, 'presently deposit your hundred pounds in gold, or else no going hence all the days of your life. I have been your physician to cure you of your queasy stomach; and here, as I deserve, I demand my fee for the same.' The abbot down with his dust; and, glad he had escaped so, returned to Reading, as somewhat lighter in purse, so much more merry in heart than when he came thence.

The only cure for old age.—Christ when on earth cured many a spot, especially of leprosy, but never smoothed any wrinkle, never made any old man young again. But in heaven he will do both (Ephes. v. 27): when 'he shall present to himself a glorious church, not having spot or wrinkle or any such thing, but that it should be holy and without blemish.' Triumphant perfection is not to be hoped for in the militant Church; there will be in it many spots and wrinkles, as long as it consisteth of sinful, mortal man.

It is Christ's work, beyond the power of man, to make a perfect reformation.

General promises of special grace.—Isaac, ignorantly going along to be offered, propounded to his father a very hard question: 'Behold the fire and the wood, but where is the lamb for the burnt-offering?' (Gen. xxii. 7). Abraham returned: 'God will provide himself a lamb for a burnt-offering.' But was not this a *gratis dictum* of Abraham? Did he not herein speak without book? Where and when did God give him a promise to provide him a lamb? Indeed he had no particular promise as to this present point; but he had a general one: 'Fear not, Abraham, I am thy shield, thy exceeding great reward' (Gen. xv. 1). Here was not only a lamb, but a flock, yea, a herd of all cattle, promised to him. It hath kept many an honest heart in these times from sinking into despair, that though they had no express Scripture that they should be freed from the particular miseries relating to these vows, yet they had God's grand charter for it. 'And we know that all things work together for good to them that love God, to them who are the called according to his purpose' (Rom. viii. 28).

Forgotten Martyrs. — God's calendar is more complete than man's best martyrologies; and *their* names are written in the book of life who on earth are wholly forgotten.

Martyrs.—If they had not been flesh and blood, they could not have been burnt; and if they had been no more than flesh and blood, they would not have been burnt.

Hope.—Hope is the only tie which keeps the heart from breaking.

www.ingramcontent.com/pod-product-compliance
Lightning Source LLC
Chambersburg PA
CBHW030607040726
47497CB00008B/2887